PRAISE FOR *THE HUNTED* AND BRIAN HAIG

"A crackling suspense novel." —*BookPage*

"A high-octane political thriller…Smart thrillers, like comets, come by only so often. If you're lucky, you get to experience something truly illuminating. Brian Haig, a master of the mystery genre, gives readers a similar treat with THE HUNTED…Based on a true story, THE HUNTED is as provocative and realistic a mystery as they come. At its core, it abounds with insider information on the KGB and the strong-armed intelligence industry. If it's a smart thriller you're looking for, Haig is your hero."
—*Fredericksburg Free Lance-Star* (VA)

"Fascinating." —*San Francisco Book Review*

"A solid writer of thrillers that mix action and character in roughly equal proportions…will capture the interest of readers who favor thrillers with political overtones. Haig has improved as a writer with every novel, and this one is his most polished." —*Booklist*

"A remarkable writer." —**Nelson DeMille**

"Fast-paced…Haig plots like a dervish."
—*Kirkus Reviews*

THE HUNTED

Also by Brian Haig

Secret Sanction
Mortal Allies
The Kingmaker
Private Sector
The President's Assassin
Man in the Middle

THE HUNTED

BRIAN HAIG

GC

GRAND CENTRAL
PUBLISHING

NEW YORK   BOSTON

This book is a work of fiction. Names, characters, places, and incidents are the product of the author's imagination or are used fictitiously. Any resemblance to actual events, locales, or persons, living or dead, is coincidental.

Grand Central Publishing
Hachette Book Group
237 Park Avenue
New York, NY 10017
Visit our website at www.HachetteBookGroup.com

Grand Central Publishing is a division of Hachette Book Group, Inc.
The Grand Central Publishing name and logo is a trademark of Hachette Book Group, Inc.

Printed in the United States of America

Originally published in hardcover by Hachette Book Group
First mass market edition, August 2010

10 9 8 7 6 5 4 3 2 1

For Lisa, Brian, Pat, Donnie, and Annie.
Dedicated to Elena.

Acknowledgments

There are always very many people to thank when a book is finally slapped on the shelves for sale. Certainly my family: Lisa, Brian, Paddie, Donnie, and Annie, who are always my inspiration, especially since the kids are all facing college, and I have to pay the bills. Also my parents, Al and Pat Haig—they are in every way absolutely wonderful parents, and I love them both.

And of course everybody at Grand Central Publishing, from top to bottom, a remarkable collection of talented people who couldn't be more helpful or exquisitely professional: Jamie Raab, the lovely, warmhearted publisher; my overwhelmingly gifted and understanding editor, Mitch Hoffman; the very forgiving pair of Mari Okuda and Roland Ottewell, who do the too-necessary patchwork of repairing the horribly flawed drafts I send and somehow, remarkably, make them readable; and Anne Twomey and George Cornell, who designed this stunning cover.

Most especially I want to thank my trusted agent and dear friend, Luke Janklow, and his family. Every writer should have an agent like Luke.

Last, I want to thank my friend and favorite writer, Nelson DeMille, who in addition to being—in my view—America's best and most entertaining author, does more to help and encourage aspiring writers get a start than anybody. When I first met Nelson he generously offered this great advice: "You will only write so many books, so do your best to make each one as perfect as you can."

He does, I try to, and I very much hope you enjoy this latest effort.

THE HUNTED

Book One:
The Heist

1

In the final days of an empire that was wheezing and lurching toward death, the aide watched his boss stare out the window into the darkness. Time was running out. The fate of the entire nation hinged on the next move at this juncture; the entire planet, possibly.

Any minute, his boss was due to pop upstairs and see Mikhail Gorbachev to deliver either a path to salvation or a verdict of damnation.

But exactly what advice do you offer the doctor who has just poisoned his own patient?

Only three short miles away, he knew, Boris Yeltsin had just uncorked and was slurping down his third bottle of champagne. Totally looped, the man was getting even more utterly hammered. A celebration of some sort, or so it appeared, though the aide had not a clue what lay behind it. A KGB operative dressed as a waiter was hauling the hooch, keeping a watchful eye on ol' Boris and, between refills, calling in the latest updates.

After seventy years of struggle and turmoil, it all came down to this; the fate of the world's last great empire hinged on a titanic struggle between two men—one ordained to go down as the most pathetically naïve general secretary ever; the other an obnoxious, loudmouthed lush.

Gorbachev was frustrated and humiliated, both men knew. He had inherited a kingdom founded on a catechism of bad ideas and constructed on a mountain of corpses. What was supposed to be a worker's paradise now looked with unrequited envy at third world countries and pondered how it had all gone so horribly wrong. How ironic.

Pitiful, really.

For all its fearsome power—the world's largest nuclear arsenal, the world's biggest army, colonies and "client" nations sprinkled willy-nilly around the globe—the homeland itself was a festering pile of human misery and material junk.

Two floors above them in his expansive office, Gorbachev was racking his brain, wondering how to coax the genie back into the bottle. Little late for that, they both knew. He had unleashed his woolly-headed liberalizing ideas—first, that asinine glasnost, then the slam dunk of them all, perestroika—thinking a blitzkrieg of truth and fresh ideas would stave off a collapse that seemed all but inevitable; inevitable to him, anyway. What was he thinking?

The history of the Soviet Union was so thoroughly shameful—so pockmarked with murders, genocide, treachery, corruption, egomania—it needed to rest on a mattress of lies to be even moderately palatable. Fear, flummery, and fairy tales—the three F's—those were the glue that held things together.

Now everything was coming apart at the seams: the Soviet republics were threatening to sprint from the union, the Eastern Bloc countries had already made tracks, and communism itself was teetering into a sad folly.

Way to go, Gorby.

On the streets below them a speaker with windmilling arms and megaphones for tonsils was working up a huge rabble that was growing rowdier and more rambunctious by the second. The bulletproof thickened windows smeared out his exact words; as if they needed to hear; as if they wanted to hear. Same thing street-corner preachers were howling and exhorting from Petersburg to Vladivostok: time for democracy; long past time for capitalism. Communism was an embarrassing failure that needed to be flushed down the toilet of history with all the other old faulty ideas. Just rally around Boris. Let's send Gorby and the last of his wrinkly old apparatchiks packing.

His boss cracked a wrinkled knuckle and asked softly, "So what do I tell Gorbachev?"

"Tell him he's an idiot. Tell him he ruined everything."

"He already knows that."

Then tell him to eat a bullet, Ivan Yutskoi wanted to say. Better yet, do us all a big favor, shove him out the window and have that spot-headed idiot produce a big red splat in the middle of Red Square. Future historians would adore that punctuation point.

Sergei Golitsin, deputy director of the KGB, glowered and cracked another knuckle. He cared less for what this idiot thought. "Tell me you've finally found where Yeltsin's money's coming from."

"Okay. We have."

"About time. Where?"

"It's a little hard to believe."

"I'll believe anything these days. Try me."

"Alex Konevitch."

The deputy director gave him a mean look. After a full year of shrugged shoulders, wasted effort, and lame excuses, the triumphant tone in his aide's voice annoyed him. "And am I supposed to know this name?" he snapped.

"Well, no... you're not... really."

"Then tell me about... what's this name?"

"Alex Konevitch." Yutskoi stuffed his nose into the thick folder, shuffled a few papers, and withdrew and fixated on one typed sheet. "Young. Only twenty-two. Born and raised in an obscure village in the Ural Mountains you've never heard of. Both parents are educators, mother dead, father formerly the head of a small, unimportant college. Alex was a physics student at Moscow University."

Yutskoi paused for the reaction he knew was coming. "Only twenty two," his boss commented with a furious scowl. "He ran circles around you idiots."

"I've got photographs," said Yutskoi, ignoring that outburst. He withdrew a few blown-up eight-by-ten color photos from his thick file and splayed them like a deck of cards before his boss. Golitsin walked across the room, bent forward, adjusted his rimless glasses, and squinted.

The shots were taken, close up, by a breathtakingly attractive female agent who had entered Konevitch's office only the day before on the pretext of looking for a job. Olga's specialty was honeypot operations, the luring of victims into the sack for entrapment or the value of their pillow talk. She could do shy Japanese schoolgirls, a kittenish vixen, the frosty teacher in need of a role reversal, a doctor, a nurse, a wild cowgirl—whatever men lusted after in their most flamboyant yearnings, Olga could be it, and then some.

Olga had never been turned down. Not once, ever.

A top-to-bottom white blonde, she had gone in attired in an aggressively short skirt, low-cut blouse—not too low, though—and braless. Olga had pitch-perfect intuition about these things: no reason to doubt her instincts now. Demure, not slutty, she had artfully suggested. A few tactful hints, but sledgehammers were to be avoided.

Alex Konevitch was a successful businessman, after all; office games were the play of the day.

A miniature broadcasting device had been hidden in her purse, and every chance she had she snapped pictures of him with the miniature camera concealed inside her bracelet. Yutskoi reached into his folder and withdrew a tape recorder. The cassette was preloaded and ready to roll. "Olga," he mentioned casually, requiring no further introduction. "She was instructed merely to get a job and learn more about him. If something else developed, well, all the better."

Golitsin jerked his head in approval, and Yutskoi set the device down on the desk and pushed play.

Golitsin craned forward and strained to hear every word, every nuance.

First came the sounds of Alex Konevitch's homely middle-aged secretary ushering Olga into his office, followed by the usual nice-to-meet-you, nice-to-meet-you-too claptrap before the game began.

Very businesslike, Konevitch: "Why do you want to work here?"

Olga: "Who wouldn't? The old system's rotten to its core and ready to collapse. The corpse just hasn't yet recognized it's dead. We all know that. This is the best of the new. I'll learn a lot."

"Previous work experience?"

"Secretarial and statistical work, mostly. There were the two years I spent working at the State Transportation Bureau, helping estimate how many bus axles we would need next year. Bus axles?... Can you believe it? I nearly died of boredom. Then the Farm Statistics Bureau, where I'm stuck now. Do you know what it's like spending a whole month trying to project the demand for imported kumquats?"

"I can't imagine."

"Don't even try." She laughed and he joined her.

Back to business, Konevitch: "Okay, now why should I want you?"

A long and interesting pause. Stupid question—open your eyes, Alex, and use a little imagination.

Olga, sounding perfectly earnest: "I type eighty words a minute, take dictation, have good phone manners, and am very, very loyal to my boss."

Another interesting pause.

Then, as if Konevitch missed the point: "I have a very capable secretary already."

"Not like me, you don't."

"Meaning what?"

"I will make you very happy."

Apparently not, because Konevitch asked quite seriously, "What do you know about finance?"

"Not much. But I'm a fast study."

"Do you have a university degree?"

"No, and neither do you."

Another pause, this one long and unfortunate.

Konevitch, in a suddenly wary voice: "How do you know that?"

"I... your receptionist..." Long pause, then with uncharacteristic hesitance, "Yes, I believe she mentioned it."

"He. His name is Dmetri."

"All right... he. I misspoke. Who cares who told me?"

Konevitch, sounding surprisingly blasé: "What gave you the idea I'm looking to hire?"

"Maybe you're not. I'm fishing. My mother is desperately ill. Throat and lung cancer. Soviet medicine will kill her, and I need money for private treatments. Her life depends on it."

Nice touch, Yutskoi thought, admiring Olga's spontaneous shift of tack. Among the few details they *had* gleaned about Alex Konevitch was that his mother had passed away, at the young age of thirty-two, of bone cancer in a state sanitarium. Like everything in this country, Soviet medicine was dreadful. Yutskoi pictured Mrs. Konevitch in a lumpy bed with filthy sheets, writhing and screaming as her bone sores oozed and burned and her young son looked on in helpless agony.

Surely that pathetic memory rushed into Alex's head as he considered this poor girl and her ailing mother. Have a heart, Alex; you have the power to save her mama from an excruciating, all but certain death. She'll twitch and suffer and cough her lungs out, and it will be all your fault.

"I'm sorry, I don't think you'll fit in."

She had been instructed to get the job, whatever it took, and she had given it her best shot and then some. Olga's perfect record was in ruins.

Yutskoi slid forward in his seat and flipped off the recorder. A low grunt escaped Golitsin's lips, part disappointment, part awe. They leaned forward together and studied with greater intensity the top photograph of Alex Konevitch taken by Olga. The face in the photo was lean, dark-haired and dark-eyed, handsome but slightly baby-faced, and he was smiling, though it seemed distant and distinctly forced.

Nobody had to coerce a smile when Olga was in the

room. Nobody. Golitsin growled, "Maybe you should've sent in a cute boy instead."

"No evidence of that," his aide countered. "We interviewed some of his former college classmates. He likes the ladies. Nothing against one-night stands, either."

"Maybe he subsequently experienced an industrial accident. Maybe he was castrated," Golitsin suggested, which really was the one explanation that made the most sense.

Or maybe he suspected Olga.

"Look at him, dressed like an American yuppie," Golitsin snorted, thumping a derisive finger on a picture. It was true, Konevitch looked anything but Russian in his tan slacks and light blue, obviously imported cotton button-down dress shirt, without tie, and with his sleeves rolled up to the elbows. The picture was grainy and slightly off-center. He looked, though, like he just stepped out of one of those American catalogues: a young spoiled prototypical capitalist in the making. Golitsin instantly hated him.

He had been followed around the clock for the past three days. The observers were thoroughly impressed. A working animal, the trackers characterized him, plainly exhausted from trying to keep up with his pace. The man put in hundred-hour workweeks without pause. He seemed to sprint through every minute of it.

Broad-shouldered, with a flat stomach, he obviously worked hard to stay in tip-top shape. Olga had learned from the receptionist that he had a black belt, third degree, in some obscure Asian killing art. He did an hour of heavy conditioning in the gym every day. Before work, too. Since he arrived in the office at six sharp and usually kicked off after midnight, sleep was not a priority. Olga had also remarked on his height, about six and a half feet, that she found him ridiculously sexy, and for once, the target was one *she* would enjoy boinking.

Yutskoi quickly handed his boss a brief fact sheet that summarized everything known to date about Alex Konevitch. Not much.

"So he's smart," Golitsin said with a scowl after a cursory glance. That was all the paucity of information seemed to show.

"Very smart. Moscow University, physics major. Second highest score in the country his year on the university entrance exam."

Alex had been uncovered only three days before, and so far only a sketchy bureaucratic background check had been possible. They would dig deeper and learn more later. A lot more.

But Moscow University was for the elite of the elite, and the best of those were bunched and prodded into the hard sciences, mathematics, chemistry, or physics. In the worker's paradise, books, poetry, and art were useless tripe and frowned upon, barely worth wasting an ounce of IQ over. The real eggheads were drafted for more socially progressive purposes, like designing bigger atomic warheads and longer-range, more accurate missiles.

Golitsin backed away from the photo and moved to the window. He was rotund with short squatty legs and a massive bulge under a recessed chin that looked like he'd swallowed a million flies. He had a bald, glistening head and dark eyes that bulged whenever he was angry, which happened to be most of the time. "And where has Konevitch been getting all this money from?" he asked.

"Would you care to guess?"

"Okay, the CIA? The Americans always use money."

Yutskoi shook his head.

Another knuckle cracked. "Stop wasting my time."

"Right, well, it's his. All of it."

Golitsin's thick eyebrows shot up. "Tell me about that."

"Turned out he was already in our files. In 1986, Konevitch was caught running a private construction company out of his university dorm room. Quite remarkable. He employed six architects and over a hundred workers of assorted skills."

"That would be impossible to hide, a criminal operation of such size and scale," the general noted, accurately it turned out.

"You're right," his aide confirmed. "As usual, somebody snitched. A jealous classmate."

"So this Konevitch was always a greedy criminal deviant."

"So it seems. We reported this to the dean at Moscow University, with the usual directive that the capitalist thief Konevitch be marched across a stage in front of his fellow students, disgraced, and immediately booted out."

"Of course."

"Turns out we did him a big favor. Konevitch dove full-time into construction work, expanded his workforce, and spread his projects all over Moscow. People are willing to pay under the table for quality, and Konevitch established a reputation for reliability and value. Word spread, and customers lined up at his door. When perestroika and free-market reforms were put in place, he cleaned up."

"From construction work?"

"That was only the start. Do you know what arbitrage is?"

"No, tell me."

"Well…it's a tool capitalists employ. When there are price differences for similar goods, an arbitrager can buy low, sell it all off at a higher price, and pocket the difference. Like gambling, he more or less bets on the margins in between. Konevitch's work gave him intimate familiarity with the market for construction materials, so this was the sector he first concentrated in."

"And this is…successful?"

"Like you wouldn't believe. A price vacuum was created when Gorbachev encouraged free-market economics. The perfect condition for an arbitrager, and Konevitch swooped in. There's a lot of construction and no pricing mechanism for anything."

"Okay."

That okay aside, Yutskoi suspected this was going over his boss's head. "Say, for example, a factory manager in Moscow prices a ton of steel nails at a thousand rubles. A different factory manager in Irkutsk might charge ten thousand rubles. They were all pulling numbers out of thin air. Nobody had a clue what a nail was worth."

"And our friend would buy the cheaper nails?" Golitsin suggested, maybe getting it after all.

"Yes, like that. By the truckload. He would pay one thousand rubles for a ton in Moscow, find a buyer in Irkutsk willing to pay five thousand, then pocket the difference."

Golitsin scrunched his face with disgust. "So this is about nails?" He snorted.

"Nails, precut timber, steel beams, wall board, concrete, roofing tiles, heavy construction equipment…he gets a piece of everything. A big piece. His business swelled from piddling to gigantic in nothing flat."

Sergei Golitsin had spent thirty years in the KGB, but

not one of those outside the Soviet empire and the impoverishing embrace of communism. Domestic security was his bread and butter, an entire career spent crushing and torturing his fellow citizens. He had barely a clue what arbitrage was, didn't really care to know, but he nodded anyway and concluded, "So the arbitrager is a cheat."

"That's a way of looking at it."

"He produces nothing."

"You're right, absolutely nothing."

"He sucks the cream from other people's sweat and labor. A big fat leech."

"Essentially, he exploits an opening in a free-market system. It's a common practice in the West. Highly regarded, even. Nobody on Wall Street ever produced a thing. Most of the richest people in America couldn't build a wheel, much less run a factory if their lives depended on it."

Golitsin still wasn't sure how it worked, but he was damned sure he didn't like it. He asked, "And how much has he...this Konevitch character...how much has he given Yeltsin?"

"Who knows? A lot. In American currency, maybe ten million, maybe twenty million dollars."

"He had that much?"

"And then some. Perhaps fifty million dollars altogether. But this is merely a rough estimate on our part. Could be more."

Golitsin stared at Yutskoi in disbelief. "You're saying at twenty-two, he's the richest man in the Soviet Union."

"No, probably not. A lot of people are making a ton of money right now." Yutskoi looked down and toyed with his fingers a moment. "It would be fair to say, though, he's in the top ten."

The two men stared down at their shoes and shared the same depressing thought neither felt the slightest desire to verbalize. If communism went up in flames, their beloved KGB would be the first thing tossed onto the bonfire. In a vast nation with more than forty languages and dialects, and nearly as many different ethnic groups, there was only one unifying factor, one common thread—nearly every citizen in the Soviet Union had been scorched by their bureau in one way or another. Not directly, perhaps. But somebody dear, or at least close: grandfathers purged by Stalin; fathers who had disappeared and rotted in the camps under Brezhnev; aunts and uncles brought in for a little rough questioning under Andropov. Something. Nearly every family tree had at least one branch crippled or lopped off by the boys from the Lubyanka. The list of grudges was endless and bitter.

Yutskoi was tempted to smile at his boss and say: I hope it all does fall apart. Five years being your bootlicker, I've hated every minute of it. You'll be totally screwed, you nasty old relic.

Golitsin knew exactly what the younger man was thinking, and was ready to reply: You're a replaceable, third-rate lackey today, and you'll be a starving lackey tomorrow. Only in this system could a suck-up loser like you survive. The only thing you're good at is plucking fingernails from helpless victims. And you're not even that good at that.

Yutskoi: I'm young and frisky; I'll adapt. You're a starched lizard, a wrinkled old toad, an icy anachronism. Your own grandchildren fill their diapers at the sight of you. I'll hire you to shine my shoes.

Golitsin: I cheated and backstabbed and ass-kissed my way up to three-star general in this system, and I'll find a way in the next one, whatever that turns out to be. You, on the other hand, will always be a suck-up loser.

"Why?" asked Golitsin. As in, why would Alex Konevitch give Yeltsin that much money?

"Revenge could be a factor, I suppose."

"To get back at the system that tried to ruin him. How pedestrian."

"But, I think," Yutskoi continued, trying to look thoughtful, "mostly influence. If the union disintegrates, Yeltsin will wind up president of the newly independent Russia. He'll owe this guy a boatload of favors. A lot of state enterprises are going to be privatized and put on the auction block. Konevitch will have his pick—oil, gas, airlines, banks, car companies—whatever his greedy heart desires. He could end up as rich as Bill Gates. Probably richer."

Golitsin leaned back and stared up at the ceiling. It was too horrible to contemplate. Seventy years of blood, strain, and sweat was about to be ladled out, first come, first served—the biggest estate sale the world had ever witnessed. The carcass of the world's largest empire carved up and bitterly fought over. The winners would end up rich beyond all imagination. What an ugly, chaotic scramble that was going to be.

"So why didn't we find out about this Alex Konevitch sooner?" Golitsin snapped. Good question. When, three years before, Boris Yeltsin first began openly shooting the bird at Gorbachev and the Communist Party, the KGB hadn't worried overly much. Yeltsin was back then just another windbag malcontent: enough of those around to be sure.

But Yeltsin was a whiner with a big difference; he had once been a Politburo member, so he understood firsthand exactly how decrepit, dim-witted, incompetent, and scared the old boys at the top were.

That alone made him more dangerous than the typical blowhard.

And when he announced he was running for the presidency of Russia—the largest, most powerful republic in the union—the KGB instantly changed its mind and decided to take him dreadfully seriously indeed.

His offices and home were watched by an elite squad of nosy agents 24/7. His phones were tapped, his offices and home stuffed with enough bugs and listening gadgets to hear a fly fart. Several agents insinuated themselves inside his campaign organization and kept the boys at the center up to date on every scrap and rumor they overheard. Anybody who entered or left Yeltsin's offices was shadowed and, later, approached by a team of thugs who looked fierce and talked even fiercer. Give Boris a single ruble, they were warned, and you'll win the national lotto—a one-way ticket to the most barren, isolated, ice-laden camp in Siberia.

Concern, not worry, was the prevailing mood among the big boys in the KGB. This was their game. After seventy years of undermining democracy around the world, they knew exactly how to squeeze and strangle Yeltsin. An election takes money, lots of it; cash for travel and aides and people to carry and spread the message across the bulging, diverse breadth of a nation nearly three times the size of America.

Boris wasn't getting a ruble. Not a single ruble. He would rail and flail to his heart's content in empty halls and be roundly ignored. After being thoroughly shellacked in the polls, he would crawl under a rock and drink himself into the grave. So long, Boris, you idiot.

It was the inside boys who first raised the alarm. Hard cash was being ladled out by the fistful to campaign employees, to travel agencies, to advertisers, to political organizers. The conclusion was disquieting and inescapable: somewhere in the shadows a white knight was shoveling money at Yeltsin, gobs of it. Boris was spending a fortune flying across Russia in a rented jet, staying in high-class hotels, and to be taken more seriously, he had even traveled overseas to America, to introduce himself to the American president; Gorby was forced to call in a big favor, but he got Boris stiffed by a low-level White House flunky before he got within sniffing distance of the Oval Office. Boris's liquor bills alone were staggering.

Millions were being spent, tens of millions. Where was the mysterious cash coming from?

A task force was hastily formed, experts in finance and banking who peeked and prodded under all the usual rocks.

Nothing.

A team of computer forensics experts burgled Boris's campaign offices and combed the deepest crevices of every hard drive.

Not a trace.

Long, raucous meetings were held about what to do, with the usual backbiting, finger-pointing, and evasion of responsibility. This sneaky white knight, whoever he was, knew how to hide his fingerprints. Whatever he was doing to evade their most advanced techniques of snooping and detection had to be enormously clever. That level of sophistication raised interesting questions and dark misgivings. After much heated discussion, inevitably the preponderance of suspicion fell on foreign intelligence agencies. Surveillance of selected foreign embassies and known intelligence operatives was kicked up a notch and the squad of watchers increased threefold. Most of the foreign embassies were wired for sound anyway. And after seventy years of foreign spies lurking and sneaking around its capital, the KGB had a tight grip on every drop site and clandestine meeting place in Moscow.

More nada.

As Yeltsin's poll numbers climbed, frustration grew. The KGB was averse to mysteries—unsolved too long they turned into career problems. So the KGB chief of residency in Washington was ordered to kick the tires of his vast web of moles, leakers, and traitors in the CIA, DIA, FBI, NSA, and any other alphabet-soup agency he had his devious fingers in. Money, cash, lucre—that was America's preferred weapon. And even if America wasn't the culprit, the CIA or NSA, with their massive, sophisticated arsenals of electronic snoops, probably knew who was.

More nada, nada, nada. More wasted time, more wasted effort, more millions of dollars flooding out of nowhere, with more supporters flocking to Yeltsin's banner.

Yutskoi observed, "Actually, it's a miracle we found out at all. Konevitch is very, very clever."

"How clever?"

"In the private construction business, nearly everything's done in cash. And nearly all of it under the table. Compounding matters, right now, we're a mix of two economies: communist and free-market. The free-market guys know we don't have a good handle on them. They're inventing all kinds of fancy new games we don't know how to play yet. It's—"

"And what game did he play?" Golitsin interrupted in a nasty tone, tired of excuses.

"Everything was done offshore. It was smuggled out in cash, laundered under phony names at Caribbean banks, and from there turned electronic. He moved it around through a lot of banks—Swiss, African, American—divided it up, brought it back together, and just kept it moving until it became untraceable and impossible to follow."

"And how did he hand it over to Yeltsin's people?"

"That's the beauty of it. Not a single ruble ever touched the Soviet banking system. That's why we never saw it." He smiled and tried to appear confident. "What we now hypothesize was that he smuggled it back in as cash and handed it over in large suitcases." The truth was, they still had no idea, though he wasn't about to confess to that.

"Then who helped him?" Golitsin immediately barked, with a sizzling stare. Another good, unanswerable question. Soviet citizens knew zilch about international banking, money laundering, electronic transactions, or how to elude detection. The Soviet banking system was backward and shockingly unsophisticated. Besides, nobody had enough money to dream of getting fancy.

Or almost nobody—the Mafiya had money by the boatload. And they were masterminds at financial shenanigans; they had tried and perfected all kinds of underhanded tricks and scams. In the most oppressive state on earth, their survival depended on keeping their cash invisible. Golitsin waved a finger at his aide's folder. "Any evidence of that?"

"None. Not yet, anyway. It doesn't mean their crooked fingers aren't in it, just that we haven't found it."

"Keep looking. It has to be there."

After a moment, and totally out of the blue, Yutskoi mentioned, "I read a term paper he wrote as a freshman, something to do with Einstein's theory of relativity."

His boss had moved back to the window, restlessly watching the loud, angry crowd down on the street. Only a few years before the whole lot would already be in windowless wagons, trembling with fear on their way to Dzerzhinsky Square. They'd be worked over for a while, then shipped off to a uranium mine in the Urals where their hair and teeth would fall out.

The old days: he missed them already.

Yutskoi interrupted the pleasant reverie. "At least I *tried* to read his paper, I should say. I barely understood a word," he mumbled. "And all those complicated equations..." He trailed off, sounding a little stunned.

"What about it?" Golitsin asked absently. The crowd below was now dancing and chanting and growing larger by the minute. He felt weary.

"I sent it off to the director of the thermonuclear laboratory at the Kurchatov Institute. He said it was one of the most brilliant treatises he had read in years. Wanted to get it published in a few very prestigious international journals. You know, show the international community Soviet science still has what it takes. When I told him an eighteen-year-old college sophomore wrote it, he called me a liar."

His boss glanced back over his shoulder. "You already told me he's smart."

"I know I did. Now I'm saying he's more than smart."

They stared at each other a moment. Golitsin said, "He's only twenty-two."

"Yes, and that's the whole point. He's not hamstrung by old ideas. Nor has he lived long enough to have his brains and ambitions squeezed into radish pulp like everybody over thirty in this country."

Lost on neither of them was the ugly irony that they

and their thuggish organ had done that squeezing. The average Russian could barely haul himself out of bed in the morning. The only social superlatives their nation boasted were the world's highest rate of alcoholism and the shortest life span of any developed nation. What a fitting tribute.

Yutskoi cleared his throat and asked, "So what will you advise Gorbachev?" He began stuffing documents and photos back into his expandable file.

Golitsin acted preoccupied and pretended he didn't hear that question. Yutskoi was an inveterate snoop and world-class gossip; if he let the cat out of the bag now, the news would be roaring around Moscow by midnight. Then again, Golitsin thought, so what? This news was too big to contain anyway. One way or another, it would be on the tip of every tongue in the world by morning. What difference would a few hours make?

He moved away from the window and ambled back in the direction of his aide. "On Gorbachev's desk is a document abolishing the Soviet Union. That jerk Yeltsin had the Congress vote on it this afternoon."

"And it passed?"

"By a landslide. If Gorbachev signs it, the Soviet Union is toast. History. Kaput."

"And if he doesn't?" asked Yutskoi, fully enlightened now about the cause of Yeltsin's drunken celebration that night: this was bound to be a bender of historic proportions. His tenders would have to pour Boris into bed. "What then?" he asked.

"What do you think will happen, idiot? We'll disband the mutinous Congress and crack down." He pointed a crooked, veiny finger through the window in the direction of the unruly crowd below. "We'll collect a few million malcontents and dissidents. Throw a million or so into the gulags. Shoot or hang a hundred or two hundred thousand to get everybody's attention."

"Won't that be fun," the aide blurted.

Golitsin shrugged. "Leave that file on Konevitch. I'll want to study him further."

Yutskoi stood and started to leave when he felt the old man's grip on his arm. "And keep me informed of what you learn about Konevitch. Spare no resources. I want to know *everything* about this young wunderkind. Everything."

2

The first team picked him up the moment he and his wife raced out the metal gate of their housing compound and stepped on the gas toward Sheremetyevo Airport. As usual, whenever the couple traveled around Moscow, a car with flashing blue lights rode in front, the shiny black armored Mercedes sedan was tucked securely in the middle, and a third car filled with heavily armed guards brought up the rear.

They followed at a discreet distance in a beaten-up rusted Lada sedan that blended in wonderfully, since it looked like all the other wretched junkheaps roaring around the streets of Moscow.

A totally excessive precaution, really. The plane tickets for the couple had been booked electronically; they knew the flight number, the departure time, his and her seat numbers, where they were going, and how long they planned to stay.

Why he was going wasn't in their briefing; nor did it matter, nor did they care. They knew why they were following him.

That's what mattered; all that mattered.

He and the Mrs. were booked in first-class side-by-side seats, and were picked up by a fresh team the instant they cleared customs and stepped onto the plane. Within moments after falling into their plush reclining seats, they ordered two flutes of bubbly and held hands as they sipped and chatted. A lovely couple, the second trail team agreed.

This new team, one male, one female, was positioned ten rows back, squished into cramped economy seats selected for the excellent view it gave them of their target. Nobody in first class ever glanced back at the deprived unfortunates in cattle class. Detection really wasn't an issue, but they worried about it anyway, and took every precaution possible. They munched on dried-out prunes, sipped bottled water, stayed quiet, and watched.

Another precaution that was totally useless, really. Wasn't like their targets could escape, flying twenty thousand feet above the earth, racing along at five hundred miles per hour.

Besides, a third team, much larger, about eight or ten people, would be in position an hour before landing at Ferihegy Airport outside Budapest.

Tedious work, but the watchers were professionals and never relaxed. They patiently spent their time hoarding mental notes that might come in handy later. Despite all the careful planning, rehearsals, and precautions, you never knew.

He, Alex Konevitch, was dressed in a superbly cut two-piece blue wool suit, obviously imported, probably from England, and just as obviously expensive. She, his wife, Elena, wore a lovely black wool pantsuit, also superbly tailored and definitely more expensive than his. From one of those faggy, la-di-da European design houses, they guessed, but the his-and-hers fancy rags were a big tactical mistake on their part. Russians and East Europeans in general are notoriously awful dressers and it set the couple apart.

After studying countless photographs of him, they agreed his likeness was a perfect match; he would be impossible to lose or misplace. His unusual height also worked heavily in their favor; even in the densest crowd, he would stick out.

No pictures of her were included in their file—a sloppy oversight in their professional judgment. What if the couple split up? What if they took separate cabs, he to his business meeting, and she maybe to a local plaza for a little noodling through stores?

They therefore focused mostly on her, collecting useful mental notes of her appearance, her distinguishing features. About his age, they estimated—possibly twenty-two, more likely twenty-four—though vastly shorter than him. Shoulder-length blonde hair, casually brushed, light on the makeup, and she really didn't need any, they both agreed. Delicious blue eyes, large, innocently doe-like, with a slightly upturned nose, and nice figure, but a little on the skinny side, in their view. All in all, though, a sweet number, very pretty, very sexy—and best of all, very difficult to miss.

They had been told little about her. Perhaps because little was known or maybe because her background was irrelevant. Why did they care?

She was with him.

That was the key.

Thirty minutes into the flight, he extended his lounger chair, unbuttoned his collar, loosened his tie, then dozed off. She handed the stewardess a few American dollars, plugged in her earphones, and intently watched a subtitled American action movie about an airplane hijacking, of all things.

He awoke from the siesta an hour later, refreshed, ready

to dig in. He turned down an offer for a meal, withdrew a thick ream of papers from his briefcase, and got down to work. The file said he was a workaholic, driven, focused, and greedy. Looked about right.

But somewhere on this flight, they were almost certain, lurked a bodyguard. Possibly two, but no more than two: of this they were nearly certain. Alex Konevitch's life was in perpetual danger in Moscow, where it was open season on bankers, entrepreneurs, and rich businessmen. Nearly seven hundred had been whacked, bombed, or kidnapped that year alone, and there were still four months to go.

But the Wild East was behind him now; or so he believed. He would relax his precautions, as he always did when he left Mother Russia in the dust. And besides, Alex Konevitch, they had been confidently informed by their employer, regarded large bodyguard detachments as distasteful, ostentatious, and worse—bad for business. A large flock of elephant-necked thugs tended to upset the Western investors and corporate types he dealt with.

But somewhere on this flight, they were quite sure, a bodyguard or bodyguards were seated, like them, calm and unobtrusive, waiting and watching. They held out little hope of detecting them, at least during the flight; these boys came from a well-heeled foreign private outfit with a first-class reputation, mostly former intelligence and police types who got paid big bucks not to make stupid mistakes. But the dismal odds aside, they were ordered to give it their best shot anyway; maybe they'd catch a lucky break. They agreed beforehand to look for anybody staring a little too possessively at Alex and his pretty little Mrs.

So the couple traded turns making idle passes through the cabin, trolling back and forth, mostly to the toilets.

There were a few young men with tough faces and thick, muscular builds, but that seemed abnormally conspicuous for an elite security firm that loudly advertised its discreetness and invisibility.

At least the bodyguards wouldn't be armed; they were sure of this. Smuggling a weapon through a Russian airport was absurdly difficult. And detection would cause a public mess, the last thing a prestigious, supposedly ethical firm needed or wanted. No, they wouldn't be that stupid.

Besides, why risk getting caught when a better alternative was available?

Far easier to have somebody meet them in Budapest and discreetly hand over the heavy artillery.

On August 19, 1991, the old boys had their last desperate fling at preserving an empire hanging by its fingernails. Gorby, who had wrought so much damage with his flailing attempts at reform, was vacationing at his Black Sea resort when a clutch of rough-looking KGB officers stormed the building and took him hostage. In Moscow, a cabal including his chief of staff, vice president, prime minister, minister of defense, and KGB chairman promptly seized the organs of government.

A few thousand troops were rushed to the capital, the state television stations were seized, and water reservoirs secured; heavily armed guards were posted in front of food distribution centers to ensure a stranglehold on the city population. Tanks were littered at strategic intersections around the government section of the city—the usual signs of a beerhall putsch in progress.

Next, the cabal convened a hasty televised press conference to introduce themselves as the saviors of communism and the union. It was a disaster. They were wrinkled, sclerotic old men, unpleasant, nasty, and afraid. And it showed. Their hands trembled, their voices quivered and shook, no facial expression registered above a fierce scowl.

Never before had they smiled at their people: why start now?

Worst of all, they appeared disorganized, feeble, nervous, and ancient—as impressions go, at that precarious, decisive moment, the wrong one to convey to a fractious, anxious nation.

To say it was a glorious gift to Boris Yeltsin, a born opportunist and addicted rabble-rouser, would be an understatement. He rallied a band of fellow flamethrowers and issued a call for all Russians to join together and battle for their freedom. A large, unruly mob flocked to the Russian Congress building, heckling and chanting and daring the men who led the coup to do something about them. The cabal had been supremely confident their good citizens would respond in the best Soviet tradition—like scared, obedient sheep. The combative show of opposition caught the old boys totally by surprise.

Half argued strenuously to slaughter the whole bunch and hang their bodies from lampposts. A fine example, a paternal warning and long overdue, too. That wet noodle Gorby had been a sorry mollycoddler. The nation had grown soft and spoiled, they insisted; a good massacre was exactly the paternal medicine needed to whip it back in shape. The more dead wimps the better.

The other half wondered if a bloody spectacle might incite a larger rebellion. They weren't morally opposed by any means. In Lenin's hallowed words, as one of them kept repeating, as if anybody needed to hear it, omelets required broken eggs. But the nation had grown a little moody toward tyrants, they cautioned. The wrong move at this brittle time and they, too, might end up swinging on lampposts. Ignore the mob, they argued; in a day or two, at the outside, the crowd would grow bored and hungry and melt into the night.

Agreement proved impossible. Kill them or ignore them? Stomp them like rodents or wait them out? The old men were cleanly divided in their opinions, so they sat and squabbled in their gilded Kremlin offices, brawling and cursing one another, drinking heavily, collectively overwhelmed by the power they had stolen.

For two sleepless days the world held its breath and watched. Boris's protestors turned rowdier and more daring by the hour. They constructed signs. They howled protest chants and hurled nasty taunts at the security guards sent to control them. They erected camps, stockpiled food, heckled and sang, and prepared to stay for the duration; the coup leaders argued more tumultuously and drank more heavily.

Despite serious attempts to scare away the press, a small pesky army of reporters had infiltrated the mob and was broadcasting the whole infuriating standoff via satellite, smuggling out photographs and earning Pulitzers by the carton. The whole mess was on display, in living color for the entire globe to see.

Yeltsin adored the spotlight, and was almost giddy at having all the world as his stage. Televisions were kept on in the Kremlin offices 24/7. The old boys were forced to sit and watch as Boris—miraculously sober for once—pranced repeatedly in front of the cameras, calling them all has-beens and wannabe tyrants, threatening to run them out of town. That clown was thumbing his nose and shooting the bird at them.

For an empire in which terror was oxygen, it was humiliating; worse, it was dangerous.

On the third day the old men had had enough. They ordered the tanks to move, scatter the rabble, and crush ol' Boris. But after three hapless protestors were mowed down, the army lost its stomach. As miscalculations go, it was a horrible one. Should've sent in the ruffians from the KGB, they realized, a little sad, a little late. Need a few bones snapped, a little blood spilled, the boys from the Lubyanka were only too happy to oblige. Soldiers, on the other hand, had no appetite for flattening their own defenseless citizens. A handful of disgusted generals threw their support behind Yeltsin. A full stampede ensued.

The coup leaders were marched off in handcuffs, tired, defeated, disgruntled old men who had bungled their last chance. And Yeltsin, caught in the flush of victory, sprinted to the cameras and declared a ban on the Communist Party: a bold gesture, the last rite for a rotten old system that had run its course. The crowd roared its approval. It was also insane, and shortly thereafter was followed by an equally shortsighted act: the complete dissolution of the Soviet Union.

With a few swipes of ink the immense empire fractured into more than a dozen different nations.

For seventy years, communism had been the ingrained order—the legal system, the governing system, the economic apparatus of the world's largest nation. Lazy, wonderfully corrupt, and spitefully inefficient as they were, its millions of servants and functionaries were the veins and arteries that braided the country together. They kept it functioning. They doled out the food and miserly paychecks, assigned housing, mismanaged the factories and farms, maintained public order, distributed goods and services, kept the trains running. A terrible, horribly flawed system, for sure. Nonetheless, it was, at least, a system.

Yeltsin had given little serious thought to what would replace it, or them. A few vague notions about democracy and a thriving free market rattled around his brain, nothing more. Apparently he assumed they would sprout helter-skelter from the fertile vacuum he created.

Worse, it quickly became apparent that Yeltsin, so brilliant at blasting the system to pieces, was clueless about gluing the wreckage back together. He was a revolutionary, a radical, a demolitionist extraordinaire. Like most of the breed, he had no talent for what came after the big bang.

But Alex Konevitch definitely did. By this point, Alex already had built a massive construction business, a sprawling network of brokerage houses to administer an arbitrage business that began with construction materials and swelled to the whole range of national commodities, and a Russian exchange bank to manage the exploding finances of his hungry businesses. Amazingly, every bit of it was accomplished under the repressive nose of the communist apparatus. Dodging the KGB and working in the shadows, somehow he had self-mastered the alchemy of finance and banking, of international business.

The nation was not at all prepared for its overnight lunge into capitalism. But Alex was not only ready he was hungry.

With killer instinct, he rushed in and applied for a license to exchange foreign currency. The existing licenses had been granted by the government of the Soviet Union; whatever permissions or licenses had been endowed by that bad memory were insolvent, not worth spit. Anyway, the spirit of the day was to privatize everything, to disassemble the suffocating state bureaucracy, to mimic the West.

After a swift investigation, it turned out Alex's banks were the only functioning institutions with adequate experience and trained executives, and with ample security to safeguard what promised to be billions in transactions. Not only was the license granted, Alex ended up with a monopoly—every dollar, every yen, every franc that came or left Russia moved through his exchange bank. Cash flooded through his vaults. Trainloads from every direction, from Western companies scrambling to set up businesses in the newly capitalist country, and from wealthy Russians pushing cash out, trying to dodge the tax collector and hide their illicit fortunes overseas.

Millions of fearful Russians lined up at the doors to park their savings in Alex's bank, which happily exchanged their shrinking rubles for stable dollars or yen or deutsche marks, whatever currency their heart desired, and let them ride out the storm.

Overnight, Alex and his senior executives were setting the national exchange rates for all foreign currencies. Heady power for a young man, not yet twenty-five years old. Also, quite happily, a gold mine.

Alex took a slice of every ruble shuttled one way or the other, only two percent, but as the mountain of cash approached billions, he scraped off millions. Then tens of millions.

He saw another rich possibility and promised twenty percent interest to any Russian willing to park their savings at his bank for one year. Reams of advertisements flooded every TV station in Russia. A striking female model was used for certain pitches. She wiggled her pliant shoulders and gyrated her sinewy hips, and in a seductive whisper purred that her boyfriend was a sexy genius: his money was earning interest. Who knew it only took a little interest to get laid? To appeal to a different segment, a handsomely aged couple stood against the backdrop of a decrepit wooden cottage and in tearful voices thanked Alex's bank for ensuring their retirement funds were not only safe but actually growing by the day. Then, flash a year forward in time, and the same old couple were shown climbing sprightly into their gleaming Mercedes sedan parked in front of a charming seaside dacha.

It was unheard of. No Soviet bank ever advertised. None offered interest, not a single kopeck. Wasn't it enough that they protected their customers' money? Why should any bank dish out the bucks for its own generosity?

The commercials were vulgar and the promise of interest bordered on criminal negligence, the Soviet-era bankers growled among themselves and to whatever reporter would listen to their gripes. But twenty percent? Okay, one or two percent, maybe; but twenty? Konevitch would pay dearly for his bluster—he'd be bankrupt before a month was out.

Millions more investors lined up at the door. Billions more rubles flooded in. Alex took the deluge and hedged and bet it all against the unstable ruble, then watched as inflation soared above a thousand percent. At the end of a year, the investors took their twenty percent cut and considered themselves lucky indeed; at least their life savings hadn't melted into half a kopeck as happened to millions of miserable others. The remainder of the spread went to Alex. Nearly ninety percent of every ruble in his savings bank was his to keep. He cleaned up.

And as the economy limped from one catastrophe

to another, as the disasters piled up, Boris reached out desperately for help. At the president's insistence, a telephonic hotline was installed between Boris and his trusted whiz kid, who seemed to have this whole capitalism thing figured out. Late-night calls became routine. A single push of the red button and the president would rail about this problem or that, long, whiny diatribes fueled by staggering amounts of liquor. Alex was a cool, sober listener; also a quick study with a mathematician's lust for numbers.

Yeltsin had little background and even less appetite for financial matters; all the economic prattle bored him to tears. Alex would talk him through the latest disaster—boil it all down to simple language—propose a reasonable solution, and Boris would pounce on his cabinet the next morning, issue a few brusque instructions, and a total meltdown would be avoided, or at least postponed for another day.

One night after a long rambling conversation about the evaporating foreign currency reserves, Yeltsin paused to catch his breath, then, seemingly out of the blue, asked Alex, "By the way, how's your house?"

"Nice. Very nice."

"Is it big?"

"Fairly large, yes. Why do you ask?"

"I heard it's huge."

"Okay, it is. Very, very big."

"How many bedrooms?"

"Six, I think. Maybe seven. Why?"

"Which is it, six or seven?"

"I honestly don't know. Could be ten for all I know. I've wandered through most of it, but there are rooms I've never seen. It was a wreck when I bought it, an old brick mansion constructed before 1917. According to local lore, it was built for a baron or maybe a wealthy factory owner to house his ten children. Poor guy. He was dragged out and executed by a Bolshevik firing squad three days after the last stud went in."

"Are you pulling my leg?"

"The bullet scars are still visible on the west side of the house. That adds a certain charm."

"And after that?"

"Well, I don't know about the early years. But the Ministry of Education owned it for decades. Occasionally it was used as a school for children of the elite, sometimes as a training center for school principals. Of course they neglected it disgracefully. The electrical wiring, even the plumbing had not been updated since it was built. The pipes were made of cast iron. Turn the spigot and chunky brown slush poured out."

"But you like it?"

Alex chuckled. "What's not to like?"

"You tell me," Boris replied.

"Not a thing. I used my own construction company to gut and rebuild with the best of everything. Voice-activated lighting, saunas in every bathroom, two mahogany-paneled elevators, the works. I even had an indoor pool installed, and a well-equipped gym. The attic is now a movie theater, twenty seats, with real popcorn machines and a ten-foot screen. A French chef and three servants live in the basement and take care of everything."

After a long moment, Yeltsin asked, in a suspiciously knowing tone, "And your wife, does she like it?"

"There are a few things she might like to change," Alex admitted, a loud understatement. Elena detested the house. He had bought and refurbished it before they met, a gift to himself after he made his first hundred million and regarded it as a neat way to pat himself on the back. A gay Paris decorator had been flown in and instructed to spare no expense. He did his best. He chartered a plane, flew around the world, slept in five-star hotels, loaded up on antiques from Asia, the Middle East, and Europe. He had drapes hand-sewn in Egypt, and furniture hand-manufactured by the best craftsmen in Korea.

As the bills piled up, Alex convinced himself that he wasn't being wasteful; it was a business expense, an unavoidable cost he couldn't do without. The big money-men from Wall Street and Fleet Street and Frankfurt did not talk business with anybody not like themselves, prosperous enough to show it off.

The house was cavernous and every nook and cranny was saturated with grandeur. But Elena liked things simple and small enough that you didn't have to shout across the room at each other. She didn't care for servants, either; she was reared to do things herself, and that's how she preferred it. If she even thought about a cup of coffee, a silver urn appeared out of nowhere. The flock of hired help violated their privacy. They made her feel guilty and spoiled.

The mansion sat on the corner of two furiously busy Moscow streets, for another thing. Traffic and pedestrians were always pausing to gawk at the impressive old home, and occasionally littered the property with letters strewn with vile curses and filthy threats. In a city populated largely with impoverished former communists—their families and few belongings suffocating in six-hundred-square-foot apartments—the newly rich and their expansive indulgences were not viewed fondly.

Any day, Elena expected a flotilla of Molotov cocktails to sail through her window.

After enough hateful letters, Alex built a small guard shack out front and posted guards around the clock to chase away disgruntled tourists. But it was, quite spectacularly, a mansion and thus a magnet for the growing breed of Moscow criminals. After two attempted break-ins, another guard shack was erected, more guards were added to the rear of the house, one was posted on the roof, and enough state-of-the-art surveillance systems were sprinkled around to give a porn studio fits of envy.

Elena began calling their home "The Fortress," without affection. Still, there was no doubt the house continued to pose serious security issues and little could be done about it.

They had had discussions, Alex and Elena. Not arguments, but mild disputes that were never settled. Elena was increasingly distressed about Alex's safety. He was famous now—more truthfully, infamous—a poster child of the gold-digging opportunists who were raking it in while most Russians slapped extra locks on their doors to keep the bill collectors at bay.

And their house was right there, on the street! A bazooka fired from a passing car could blast them all to pieces.

But the place was perfect for Alex. His office was only five minutes away, on foot. He was working twenty-hour days, seven days a week. Seconds were precious, minutes priceless. And everything he needed was right here, a floor or two above, or a floor or two below: a gourmet feast at the snap of a finger, that superb gym for his morning conditioning, the heated pool to unwind in after a long day of shoving millions around.

Elena had been raised in the country. She loathed the

city and all its appendages—senseless crime, roaring traffic, the ever-present noise, the reeking smell and pollution. Most of all, she hated that disgruntled people walked by and spat angry hawkers on her property. She longed for clean air, lush forests, long, private walks around her property.

Long walks without a squadron of beefy guards shepherding her every step.

"Why do you ask?" Alex finally said.

"I want you closer," Boris replied. "No, I *need* you closer."

"I'm only forty minutes away. Call and I'll drop everything."

"Nope, that won't work. One minute I worry about foreign currency reserves, the next I'm dreaming of ways to get my nuclear missiles back from Kazakhstan. I'm a very spontaneous person, Alex. I have the attention span of a horny Cossack. I think you know that."

"Yes, I know that. So send a fast helicopter for me, Mr. President. The army's not doing anything these days. I think they have enough of them, and their pilots need a workout. I'll even foot the gas bill. Twenty minutes flat from my doorstep to yours."

"Not fast enough."

"Then describe fast enough."

"I want to reach out and touch you. Besides, you've been very good to me. I owe you more than I can express. Do me a favor, let me pay some of it back."

"Just fix this damned country. Finish what you started. Believe me, I'll be more than delighted."

Yeltsin chuckled. "You'll be old and senile before anything works in this land. I'll be dead and buried, with throngs of people lining up to pee on my grave for causing all this chaos. I'm giving you a house, Alex."

"I have a house already. Didn't we just go over that?"

Yeltsin ignored him. "Not quite as garish as yours. But big, and believe me, you'll love this place. It's out here, in the country, inside the presidential compound. A mere two-minute walk from my quarters—one minute if you sprint, which I expect you to do if I call. A gym and indoor pool. Six servants, a chef, and—hey, you'll love this part—they have separate quarters outside the house."

The president paused to let his sales pitch sink in, then threw out a little more ammunition. "Here's the kicker, Alex. My presidential security detail guards the entire compound. Even with your money, you couldn't touch the kind of security these goons provide."

Alex chuckled. "Is that a challenge?" He could not say it, but he abhorred the idea of living in walking, or even sprinting, distance of Boris. The man drank and partied until four every morning, frothy bacchanalias that consumed enormous amounts of liquor. He was notoriously social by nature and regarded it as sinful to get tanked alone. The idea of being dragged into those late-night orgies was appalling.

Yeltsin chuckled as well, then a loud belly laugh. What was he saying? With all that wealth, Alex could probably buy half the Russian army; maybe all of it. After a moment the laughing stopped. "I'm serious, Alex. My economic advisors are all boring idiots. Even that bunch of Harvard professors who've camped out here to tell me how to build a capitalist paradise—just stuffier idiots."

"All right, replace them."

"You're not listening. I'm trying to."

But Alex was listening, very closely. A week before he and Elena had attended a dull state dinner to honor the visiting potentate of some country where, apparently, everybody was short and squat, with bad teeth, horrible breath, and nauseating table manners. After the usual tedious speeches about eternal brotherhood and blah, blah, blah—along with a seriously overcooked meal—the party shifted to the ballroom, where Yeltsin promptly invited Elena to dance.

Boris had an eye for the ladies and Elena in a baggy sweatsuit could snap necks. But attired as she was, in a gold-embossed scarlet gown, she nearly sucked the male air out of the ballroom. And of course, three-quarters of a lifetime of ballet training had made her a splendid dancer who knew how to make her partner look graceful and better than he was. Yeltsin and Elena laughed and chatted and whirled gaily around the floor. All eyes were on them—Fred and Ginger, cutting the rug. One dance turned into two, then three.

Alex was sure he was listening to the echo of that third dance. Clearly Elena had whispered into Yeltsin's ear her growing concerns about Alex's safety. If her husband wouldn't heed her warnings, she would take matters over his head. He admired the effort and adored her for trying. He had absolutely no intention of humoring her.

He would just litter a few more guards around the property and hope it settled her nerves.

"Oh, one other thing," Yeltsin added, an afterthought, an insignificant little note to round out the pitch. "It happens to be Gorbachev's old house. The official quarters of the general secretary himself. I had him booted out the day after I took over. Didn't even give him time to clear the clothes from the closets. Ha, ha, ha. Had those shipped to him, later, with a nice personal note. 'I got the country, you keep the rags.'"

Alex suddenly went speechless. Had he heard that

right? Yes! Gorbachev's home! Sure, his own mansion was grand, perhaps larger and more loaded with extravagances than the general secretary's residence—money, after all, was the great leveler. But some things money can't buy. Yeltsin was offering him the most storied home in Russia.

The thought of living in that home—How may bedrooms did Yeltsin mention? Who cared?—the thought of him and Elena basking in the general secretary's hot tub, making love in that bedroom, taking long, leisurely strolls around a property where legions of presidents and world leaders had stepped and stumbled, was simply exhilarating. Flushing the toilets would be a thrill.

It wouldn't hurt business, either. Alex could picture the amazed expressions of the Western investors he invited over for a light business dinner. Please don't chip the general secretary's china, he would tell them and watch their faces.

And so what if it was forty-five minutes from the office? The big Mercedes 600 was equipped with an office in the rear, a pull-down desk made of mahogany, a satellite carphone, enough gadgets that not one of the forty-five minutes would be idle or wasted. It might even be better, he thought: forty-five minutes of solitude, each way. Organize his thoughts on the way in; unwind from the daily turmoil on the way out.

And it was safe. Plus, it was in the country; Elena would love it.

Mistaking Alex's prolonged silence for indecision, Yeltsin prattled on. Like the politician he was, he couldn't stop selling. "Let me tell you, my boy, hell, I'd dearly love to live in it myself. Sometimes, at night, Naina and I wander around that house and dream of moving in. The chandeliers alone cost more than I make in a year. Of course, word would inevitably leak out to all these poor folk scraping by on a hundred rubles a month. There'd be another revolution. You know what, though? I don't think I'd enjoy this one as much as the last."

"My moving van will be there first thing in the morning," Alex blurted. He was too stunned to say "thanks."

Matching his speed, Yeltsin snapped, "Good, glad that's settled."

"It's definitely settled. Don't you dare make this offer to anyone else before nine o'clock tomorrow. By then, Elena and I will be seated on the front porch with shotguns to drive off the interlopers."

"Oh, one other thing. From now on, I want you along when I travel overseas. Russia needs as much money and foreign investors as we can get. I'm miserable at making that happen. You don't seem to have any problems in that department."

"Sure, whatever," Alex mumbled, dreaming of who to invite over first. Would they need furniture? Where would they get groceries? In his mind he was already moved in.

The instant they signed off, he rushed upstairs, awoke Elena, and broke the news about their incredible new home.

"Oh, isn't that wonderful," she replied, even managing to make the pretense of making her surprise look sincere.

At one o'clock, Bernie Lutcher crunched hard on his third NoDoz tablet and quickly washed it down with the bottled water he had carried onto the plane.

After twenty-five years as a successful cop in the NYPD intelligence bureau, retiring as a highly regarded lieutenant, he was now five years into his second life, five years that were nearly everything he hoped they would be.

The English security firm that employed him, Malcolm Street Associates, paid him one hundred grand a year, plus housing, plus car, *and* the chance for a twenty thousand annual bonus. Four for four in the bonus department, thus far. And the way this year was going, next year's was already in the bag and mentally spent. Supplemented by his NYPD pension, he was finally and faithfully putting away a little nest egg.

But not *exactly* as he always dreamed it would be. Cancer had struck five years before, had stolen his beloved Ellie, and only after it wiped out the paltry savings they had managed to scrimp from a meager cop's salary. His medical insurance had handled the prescribed treatments, but in the final months and weeks, as Ellie stubbornly wasted away, Bernie had thrown good money after bad, desperately investing in a plethora of unorthodox treatments and quackery, from Mexican miracle pills to an oddball dentist who swore that removing Elle's silver and mercury fillings would incite a complete remission. To no avail, it turned out. In the end, Elle had passed away, stuffed with all manner of phony cures and big holes in her teeth.

So now Bernie was rebuilding his life. No longer surviving one miserable day at a time, he was again viewing life as a promising future rather than a sad past. Both kids were grown, out of college, out on their own; the first grandkid was in the oven, and Bernie looked forward to many more.

Plus, he was living in Europe. Europe! He had acquired this dream in his late teens when Uncle Sam borrowed a few years of his life, making him a military policeman in Heidelberg, a gorgeous city in a lovely country that captured his heart. Other NYPD types had Florida fever; they dreamed of sweating out their idle years in tropical heat, blasting little white spheres around manicured lawns. Bernie hated golf, hated heat, and desperately hated the idea of spending his sunset years reliving the good old days—what was so good about them, anyway?—in a community saturated with retired cops. He had always yearned to return to Europe: the slower pace, the opportunity to travel, sip exotic coffees, and of course, the money was fantastic.

He hunched forward in his seat and noted, once again, the same wrinkled old biddy lurching and waddling down the aisle toward the lavatory. He had long ago learned not to ignore anything—not the innocuous, not the apparently innocent. The stakeout king, the boys in the NYPD had nicknamed him, with good reason—he had put more than a few banditos in the slammer by paying unusual attention to cars and pedestrians that appeared a little too often, often stickup artists and bank robbers reconning their targets. Pattern observation, it was called in the trade. Bernie wrote the book on it.

This was her fifth potty trip, by his count. A little suspicious: she did look old, though, and faulty kidneys couldn't be ruled out; or doctor's orders to keep her blood circulating; or just plain old-age restlessness.

In preparation for this job, the firm's experts had produced a thick folder detailing all known and presumed threats to the client. It was a wealthy firm with a big ego that could afford to be comprehensive and took it to the hilt.

Background checks were de rigueur for all prospective clients; unlike other firms, however, this was accomplished *before* a contract was signed. The client's ability to pay the firm's impressive bills was the principal topic of curiosity, of course. Also the nature of the client's business, types of threat, known enemies, special circumstances, and bothersome vulnerabilities.

British snobbery definitely weighed in. Unsavory clients were blackballed no matter how much they pleaded or offered.

But in a ferociously competitive business, reputation counted for everything. It all boiled down to two simple questions: How many lived? How many died?

The firm had dodged more than a few bullets by politely and firmly snubbing clients whose chance of survival was deemed subpar; in over thirty percent of those cases, the clients had been dead within a year, a striking piece of guesswork. A clutch of actuarial wizards lured from top insurance firms were paid a small fortune to be finicky. A computer model was produced, a maze of complex algorithms that ate gobs of information and spit out a dizzying spread of percentages and odds.

A client or two were lost every year, a better than average record for work of this nature, one the firm loudly advertised.

Regarding his current client, at the top of the threat chain were the usual suspects for a Russian tycoon: Mafiya thugs, hit men, and various forms of independent crooks or assassins intent on blackmail, or fulfilling a contract from a third party. They were effective and often lethal. They were also crude, obnoxiously brutal, notoriously indiscreet, and with their clownish affectation for black jeans and black leather jackets, usually ridiculously easy to spot. Bernie had already swept the cabin twice. No likely suspects of that ilk.

Next came business competitors who stood to benefit by eliminating an entrepreneurial juggernaut like Konevitch, followed closely by investors disgruntled for any number of reasons. His business was privately owned. Two limited partners, that was it. He owned eighty percent of the shares and neither partner was dissatisfied, as best the firm could tell. Really, how could they be? Konevitch had made them both millionaires many times over.

His estimated worth—a combination of cash and stock—now hovered around 350 million dollars—in all likelihood a lowball estimate—and growing by the hour, despite generous and frequent contributions to local charities and political causes. He had his fingers deeply into four or five mammoth businesses, was contemplating a move into two or three more, and his personal fortune was multiplying by the day. The construction firm he began had given birth to an arbitrage business—initially for construction materials only, then for all sorts of things—that bred a prosperous bank, then a sizable investment firm, part ownership in several oil firms, a car importing company, a real estate empire, ownership of two national newspaper chains, several restaurant chains, and myriad smaller enterprises that were expected to balloon exponentially as Russia fully morphed into a full-blown consumer society.

As fast as Alex made money, he poured it into the next project, the next acquisition, the next promising idea. Whatever he touched spewed profit, it seemed. In the estimation of the firm, that remarkable growth rested firmly on his own deft brilliance, his own impeccable instincts, his golden touch.

Take him out and Konevitch Associates would fold. Maybe not immediately, maybe it would limp along for a few anguished years. But with the brain dead, the body would atrophy. Eventually the pieces would shrivel and be sold off for a fraction of a pittance. Alex was a money-printing machine; surely his partners knew this.

Next came possible political enemies, and last, though not insignificantly, the obligatory threat for anyone with heaps of money—family members who might hunger for an inheritance and/or an insurance windfall.

Nearly all rich people dabbled in politics to a greater or lesser degree; this client was in it up to his neck. According to the dossier, Konevitch was very close to Yeltsin, had apparently backed his rise to the presidency, and he continued to throw cash by the boatload at Yeltsin's hungry political machine and a few of the reformist parties ambling in his wake.

The old commie holdovers were resentful, angry, and plentiful. Konevitch had played it smart and hid in the background—the mint behind the throne, an underground well of money—going to great lengths to keep his contributions invisible, or at the very least anonymous. But there were those who knew. And among them, it was assumed, were some powerful people who might wish to settle a historical score. A nasty political grudge couldn't be ruled out.

He had a serious ten million dollar term life policy with Carroythers & Smythe, a financially plump, highly regarded insurance company. That firm shared Malcolm Street Associates' intense concern for Alex's health and secretly informed its partner agency that his wife was the sole beneficiary. No brothers, no sisters, and his few cousins were distant, angry, avid communists, and unfriendly. His mother was long dead, leaving just a father, a former educator with few apparent wants and needs, who was wiling away his retirement from academia reading books that were formerly banned to Soviet readers.

Using his vast riches, the son set the old man up in a nice dacha in a resort town on the Black Sea with a tidy trust fund that would allow him to comfortably live out his life in pleasant surroundings. A bribe to the local hospital revealed the old man had incurable pancreatic cancer that was expected, shortly, to kill him. He was being treated with the best medicines imported from the States, but few had ever survived pancreatic cancer and time was not on his side. So what would the old man want with his son's fortune? Wasn't like he could take it with him.

Alex dutifully visited every few months. He and the old man spent hours in the garage, tinkering on old jalopies and knocking back imported beers. An odd relationship, given the wild differences between father and son. But they were close.

So it all boiled down to one intimate threat—his wife, Elena.

The firm had quietly observed their marriage: happy, healthy, and loving, or so it appeared. No indications of affairs or dalliances or even one-night regrets. Not for her, not for him. They had met a year and a half earlier. And from the best they could tell, from the opening instant, the couple could barely keep their hands off each other. A surface background check revealed that she had been a dancer, Bolshoi-trained. And though marvelously talented, with a technique that was deemed technically flawless, at only five foot and one inch she lacked the long limbs and extended torso demanded by audiences. She was offered a position as a full-time instructor, teaching giraffes with half her talent to prance and pirouette; she opted, instead, to retire her tutu. She put dance in the rearview mirror and majored in economics at Moscow University, graduating five down from the top of her class. Bright girl.

A month after they met he had asked and she agreed, he suggesting a quick and efficient civil rite, she arguing vehemently for a traditional church wedding. She won and they were joined together, till death do they part, in a quiet ceremony by a hairy, bearded patriarch at a small, lovely Orthodox chapel in the pastoral countryside.

The firm regarded her fierce insistence on a church wedding as a hopeful sign—she had apparently been raised a closet Christian during the long years of godless communism; presumably, the sixth commandment meant something to her.

Her tastes were neither extravagant nor excessive. Some expensive clothing and a few costly baubles, though not by choice and definitely not by inclination: an outwardly prosperous image was necessary for business, he insisted, and he encouraged her to buy half of Paris. Day to day, she preferred tight American Levi's and baggy sweat-shirts, limiting herself to a few elegant outfits that were mothballed except for social and business occasions. The couple never bickered, never fought. They enjoyed sex, with each other, nothing kinky, nothing weird, and it was frequent. The firm knew this for a fact.

The Konevitch apartment had been wired and loaded with enough bugs to fill an opera house, surreptitiously, of course, the day after Alex first contacted Malcolm Street Associates. All married applicants were electronically surveilled, at least during the opening weeks or months of a contract—this was never divulged to the clients, and the firm's prurience had never been discovered. Since part of its service was to sweep for listening and electronic devices, it would never be caught.

Statistically, the firm knew, a high number of rich men were murdered by their own wives, concubines, and mistresses. The reasons were mostly obvious: marital neglect, sexual jealousy, and, more often, outright greed. Nothing was harder to protect against, and the actuarial boys demanded a thorough investigation. The firm's gumshoes enthusiastically obliged; snooping in the bedrooms of the rich and famous, after all, was definitely more entertaining work than the normal tedium of tailing and watching.

But all evidence indicated that the marriage was strong. And Elena Konevitch, for now and for the foreseeable future, was rated low risk.

In January 1992, the first of what soon became a flood of newspaper stories about the amazing and mysterious Alex Konevitch appeared in the *Moscow Times*. Though other newly minted Moscow tycoons begged to be noticed, pleaded for publicity, actually, Alex had prodigiously tried his best to remain a complete nobody. Other fat cats blustered and bribed their way into every hot nightspot in town, rolling up in their flashy, newly acquired Mercedes and BMW sedans, a stunning model or two hanging on their arm—typically rented for the occasion—only too hungrily enthusiastic to strut the fruits of their newfound success, to show off their sudden importance.

Publicity management firms sprang up all over Moscow. Moguls and wannabe moguls lined up outside their doors, throwing cash and favors at anybody who could get them noticed, a few seconds of limelight, the briefest mention in the local rags. Under the old system everybody was impoverished, with little to brag about, and even less to show off; in any event, sticking one's head up was an invitation to have it lopped off. Now a whole new world was emerging from the ashes; old desires that had been cruelly repressed were suddenly unchained, flagrantly indulged. A thousand egos swelled and flourished, giddy with the impulse to show off. Donald Trump was their icon; they longed to live his life, to emulate his oversized image, to become famous simply for being obnoxiously famous.

Alex lived like a hermit, a man few knew and nobody knew well. He avoided parties and nightclubs, was rarely observed in public, and adamantly refused any and all requests for interviews. In his quest to remain anonymous, every employee of Konevitch Associates and its sprawling web of companies was required to sign a serious legal vow never to whisper a word about their reclusive employer. This only made the search for his story all the more irresistible. One of the richest men in the country, the kid millionaire they naturally called him. And he wanted to remain anonymous?

After several unfruitful attempts, a midlevel employee at his investment bank was secretly approached by a Moscow weekly and offered five thousand easy American dollars to chat a little about his employer. The employee confessed that he not only did not know Alex personally, he had actually seen him only twice in person—two fleeting glimpses of Alex speeding through the trading floor on his way to his office upstairs. Didn't matter, they assured him. Surely Alex's companies were rife with rumors, gossip, and anecdotes, concocted or otherwise. The price was kicked up to seven thousand and the employee was suddenly too eager to cough up a few confidences—as long as the check was good and, for sure, his name stayed out of it.

"Kid Midas" was the predictable headline that outed Alex, and it said it all and then some. It was rumored that

Alex was Russia's richest man, its first fat-cat billionaire; he owned an armada of towering yachts; two hundred rare and exotic sports cars housed in a temperature-controlled underground garage and spitshined daily; a fleet of sleek private jets to ferry him to his sprawling estates in Paris, London, Rome, New York, and Hong Kong. The chatty employee had recently finished a spicy, newly translated, unauthorized biography about the marvelously perverse life of Howard Hughes, and he plagiarized liberally and imaginatively from that intoxicating tale to earn his seven grand.

Alex was a total schizoid paranoid, he'd said; he sat around his office nude, counting his rubles and hatching new businesses in between watching old black-and-white Katharine Hepburn flicks. He collected beautiful women by the carton, renamed them all Katharine, and was so germophobic that he boiled them before he slept with them. He was anti-Semitic, antisocial, ate only raw vegetables, drank only boiled water, was left-handed, was rumored to go both ways sexually, and had to be chloroformed by a squad of brawny assistants to get haircuts and his fingernails trimmed.

The resulting article was ridiculous, packed with bizarre lies, and viciously fascinating.

Fictitious or not, it incited an all-out frenzy and induced scores of Moscow reporters to join in the hunt. Sensationalized stories about Alex quickly became daily fare, more often than not outrageously fabricated nonsense. One enterprising weekly magazine initiated a column dubbed "Kid Midas Sightings" so the whole city could join in the fun: a five hundred dollar reward was offered to anybody who could produce a photograph of Alex, five thousand if he was nude, purportedly his normal state.

Alex's attorneys begged him to sue, promising to terrorize the publishing industry, as only lawyers can do. A flat, persistent refusal was his stubborn response. It would only generate more unwanted publicity, he insisted. And anyway, it was a novelty that would quickly wear off, he assured them, but he promptly hired his first security people. Six private bodyguards. All former Spetsnaz special forces warriors, who looked fierce and swore they would be loyal to the end.

Alex was still scribbling notes and poring over thick business files when, two hours later, the pilot's nasal voice launched the usual preparatory steps for landing. Seat backs were jolted forward, eating trays shoved back into position, a few people got up and stretched. The pair of watchers exchanged knowing winks.

Time for the fun to begin.

They followed Mr. and Mrs. Konevitch as they deplaned, he hauling their leather overnight bags casually slung over his broad shoulders; both of them totally clueless. Light packing for what the couple obviously assumed would be a brief and enjoyable business trip, in and out, a single night at most. Guess again, Alex.

The carry-on luggage was a welcome relief, nonetheless. Their instructions were stern and clear: avoid loose ends, anything that might make the authorities suspicious. The Hungarian police weren't known for nosiness or efficiency. Interference seemed unlikely. Still, unclaimed bags that were tagged with contact information might cause an unwanted problem or two.

At customs, Mr. and Mrs. Konevitch offered polite smiles to the green-uniformed customs guard, flashed their Russian passports, no problems there. Then they went directly through the sliding glass doors into the expansive lobby.

Midday. The foot traffic was sparse, which made the targets easy to track, but also made it harder for the reception team to blend in and hide.

Their briefing was unequivocal on this point—stay with the Konevitches every second of every minute. No respite until the arrival-and-reception team had matters firmly in hand. Same kind of job they had done hundreds or possibly thousands of times during the past fifty years, always successfully. Old age had slowed them down a few steps, but in their line of work the trade-off was more than equitable; nobody suspected a pair of doddering old geezers.

The customs agent barely gave them or their passports a glance as he waved them through. What possible threat could these wrinkled old wrecks pose to the Republic of Hungary? they were sure he was thinking. If only he knew. They had thirty confirmed kills to their credit, with six more they stubbornly claimed, though the corpses had been incinerated into ashes or fallen into deep rivers and washed away.

Mr. and Mrs. Konevitch were walking briskly through the lobby, straight for the taxi stand outside. The tail team followed at a safe distance, hobbling and creaking with every step.

At the taxi stand, three people were already lined up ahead of the Konevitches—a hatchet-faced lady struggling with her oversized luggage, and two faces the tails instantly recognized, Vladimir and Katya.

Vladimir was the boss of the arrival-and-reception team, a man they all thoroughly feared and deeply loathed. Katya, like the rest of them, was vicious, cold-blooded, and unemotional, a veteran killer with a long and enviable list of hits—but always just business. Vladimir was a sadistic bastard with freakish appetites. He would've done this work for free; paid to do it, probably. Even the toughest killers in the unit felt a wash of pity for his victims.

The tail team from the airplane backed off, ignoring the Konevitches and redirecting their attention to trying to spot the private bodyguards. They had memorized as many faces from their flight as they could. Now they separated from each other, about twenty yards apart, stopped, pretended to fumble with their luggage, and watched for familiar faces.

The call came in at 2:37 p.m. and the secretary put it right through.

Sergei Golitsin checked his watch, right on time. He lifted the phone and barked, "Well?"

"Good news, they're here," the voice informed him. "Everything's under control."

"So you have them?"

"No, not yet. They're at the taxi stand two feet from Vladimir and Katya. Everything's on schedule, everything's in place. I'll call you in a few minutes when we do."

"Don't mess this up." Golitsin snorted.

"Relax. We won't."

There was a long pause. Golitsin, with barely suppressed excitement, asked, "Are the communications set up?"

"They are. The listening devices are state of the art. You'll get a crystal-clear feed into the phone lines and through your speakerphone. I tested it with your secretary an hour ago. Everything's fine." After a pause, the voice added, "Vladimir's going to handle this. It's going to be loud and ugly."

"It better be." Golitsin closed his eyes and smiled. "I want to hear every sound."

3

The old lady at the front of the line shoved two bags at a cabbie and crawled painfully into a blue BMW with TAXI splashed in bold letters across the side.

The couple directly in front of Alex and Elena stepped forward, and a black Mercedes sedan that had been idling by the far curb suddenly swerved in front of the other taxis and screeched to a noisy halt half a foot from the taxi stop. Vladimir, wearing the garb and collar of a Catholic priest, made a fast survey of the surroundings, then quickly threw open the rear door. The same instant, Katya, dressed as a nun, pushed out an ugly black pistol hidden inside the folds of her baggy sleeve and pointed it in Alex's face.

Her partner turned around. Coldly and in Russian he said to Alex, "It's a simple choice. Get into the car or die right here and right now."

Alex looked into his eyes. He had not the slightest doubt he meant every word. After a moment, he said, "Fine, I'll go. This young lady, however, you will leave alone. I don't know her. She's not with me."

"Don't be stupid, Konevitch. Katya will kill you, or your wife, or both of you. Doesn't matter to us."

Alex's face froze. His *name*. The man had used his name, and he *knew* Elena was his wife. For three years he had prepared himself for a moment like this. Dreamed about it. Dreaded it. Now it was actually happening, and he couldn't think or react.

Vladimir's thick hands shot out and grabbed Elena by the neck. He spun her around like a puppet; one hand slipped under her chin, the other against the back of her head. Elena squirmed and fought at first, but Vladimir was too large and strong. He tightened his grip, and she yelped with pain.

Vladimir said to Alex, "You have a black belt, I hear. Surely you recognize this stance. A quick shift of my weight and her neck will snap like a rotten twig. Now, will you *please* get into the cab?"

As they were sure he would, without hesitation or another word, Alex climbed inside. A moment later, Elena was shoved in beside him and landed awkwardly against his side. The man knew what he was doing; he was using her as a buffer from Alex's hands, and he squeezed into the backseat to her right. The woman in the nun's outfit, obviously anything but one of God's saintly servants, slipped into the front passenger seat with her pistol in Alex's face.

The driver, a trusted cohort and a skilled getaway man, gunned the engine, popped the clutch, and off they sped with a noisy screech. Nobody said a word. As if on cue, the lady in the front shifted her gun at Elena's face. The man in priest's garb said to Alex, "Hold up your hands, together."

Alex did as he was told. The man bent across Elena and efficiently slapped thick plastic cuffs on Alex's wrists, then with a show of equal dexterity, Elena's.

After a moment, Alex asked, "What do you want?"

"Be quiet," came the reply from Vladimir. He withdrew two black hoods and clumsily covered their heads.

*   *   *

In March 1992, two months after the press frenzy over
Alex Konevitch began, the initial attacks on his companies were detected.

Somebody was making repeated highly sophisticated
attempts to break into Konevitch Associates' computer net-
works. Quite successfully, or so it appeared. The Russian
Internet backbone, like everything inherited from communism, was shockingly backward and inefficient. Alex
had therefore hired an American company that specialized
in these things and plowed millions into creating his own
corporate network, a closed maze of servers, switches,
and privately owned fiber-optic cable that connected his
companies. The only vulnerabilities were in the interfaces
between his private network and the Russian phone companies, interfaces that were, regrettably, unavoidable. Naturally this was precisely where the attacks occurred.

That discovery was made minutes after a new American anti-virus software program was installed, a magical
sifter that sorted gold from fool's gold. Tens of thousands
of spyware programs were detected—like small track-
ing devices—that had penetrated and riddled the entire
network. The programs were sophisticated little things,
impossible to detect with homegrown software. They not
only tracked the flow of Internet traffic, they caused each
message to replicate and then forwarded copies to an outside Internet address.

Private investigators easily tracked the Internet address
to a small apartment on the outer ring of Moscow and
burgled their way into the flat. It was completely empty
and wiped clean. Nothing, except a small table and dusty
computer. The plug was pulled out. The hard disk had
been removed.

What was going on? Alex had anxiously queried his technical specialists. Somebody is mapping your businesses and transactions, came the answer. For how long? he asked. Maybe weeks, more probably months, and it seemed fair to conclude that whoever launched this attack now had an avalanche of information regarding how his rapidly expanding empire came together, how one piece interfaced with the next, how and where the money flowed, even the identities of the key people who pushed the buttons. The computers in the human resources department, particularly, were riddled with enough spyware to feed a software convention.

The programs were wiped clean, gobs of money were thrown at more protective software—all imported from America, all state of the art, all breathtakingly expensive—and nothing was heard from the originator of the attack. Corporate extortion or any of several forms of embezzlement had been anticipated—pay us off, the intercepted traffic will be destroyed, the attacks will stop. But after long weeks during which Alex's hired computer wizards held their breath and nobody approached the firm, a new, more hopeful scenario was reached. It was probably one of the expanding army of nettlesome computer nerds, his technical people speculated—nothing to be overly concerned with. This was an everyday problem in the United States, Alex was told, where hackers sat up all night and thought up ways to be bothersome for no greater reason than the idiotic satisfaction of imagining it made them something more than the insignificant little twits they were.

In fact, Alex was warned, it could have been much worse; the sneaks could've hacked in, crashed the entire system, and demolished mounds of irreplaceable

information. A helpful and timely warning, actually—
take better precautions, spend whatever it takes, and then
some. Stay alert. Be thankful we detected the problem
early and eliminated it, Alex was told by his head technician, an American imported and paid a small fortune for
his erudition in these matters.

4

The old lady was merely daft, Bernie Lutcher concluded, at first.

She had jumped in front of him, repeating something loudly in Russian. At least it sounded like Russian. He understood not a word and shrugged his shoulders, and she switched to a different tongue, more quick bursts of incomprehensible gibberish—possibly Hungarian now— while he continued to shrug and tried to brush past her. To his rising impatience, she clutched his arm harder and ratcheted up the incoherent babble.

He recalled her from the plane, the old lady with apparent incontinence issues who made trip after trip to the potty. Maybe she was seeking directions to the air terminal ladies' room, he guessed. Or maybe she was a certified loony, a lonely human nuisance of the type found in every city in the world.

He tried to tug his arm away again and noticed how surprisingly strong she was. Ahead, he watched Alex and Elena pass through the electronic doors, and felt a sudden clutch of alarm. Depending on the length of the line outside, it might take only a few seconds for them to climb into a taxi and disappear into the vast, winding labyrinth of Budapest streets.

He knew their schedule and the name of their hotel: he could always catch up with them there. Unfortunately, he

was pathologically honest and duty-bound to enter any
coverage lapses in the report he assiduously completed
and turned in after each job. In his mind he had already
spent his annual bonus on a nice holiday in Greece, on a
luxurious slow cruise through the sunbaked islands, sip-
ping ouzo and ogling Scandanavian tourist girls in their
Lilliputian bikinis; he now was watching it all go up in
smoke.

He tried to recall any fragment of every language
he knew and quickly blurted at the old lady, "Excuse
me... *entschuldigen...excusez-moi...por favor...*" Nothing, no relief.

A large crowd began catching up to him, impatient
travelers who had just cleared customs and now were
plowing ahead and jostling for choice spots in the taxi
line. He could hear their voices, but kept one eye on the
old lady—who clutched his arm harder and acted increasingly distressed—and the other on the glass door Alex
and Elena had just exited. He never turned around, never
observed the old man who quickly approached his back.

The old lady continued prattling about something, more
loudly frantic now, more mysteriously insistent, still stubbornly clasping his arm. Firm procedures were unequivocal
about such situations: public scenes and embarrassments,
indeed public attention in any form, were to be avoided
at all costs. He reached down and gently tried to pry his
arm loose from the old hag's grip, even as an old man
approached from his rear aggressively swinging his arms
with each step. Gripped tightly in the old man's right hand,
and mostly obscured by an overly long coat sleeve, was a
razor-thin, specially made thirteen-inch dagger.

One step back from the bodyguard's rear, it swung
up. The blade entered Bernie Lutcher's back nearly six

inches below his left shoulder blade, grazed off one rib, then immediately penetrated his heart.

The old man gave it a hard grind and twist, a signature technique honed decades before, one he was quite proud of, tearing open at least two heart chambers, ensuring an almost immediate death. In any event, the blade was coated with a dissolvable poison primed to instantly decrystallize and rush straight into Bernie's bloodstream. One way or another, he'd be dead.

Bernie's eyes widened and his lips flew open. At the same instant, the old lady gave him a hard punch—an expertly aimed blow to the solar plexus to knock the wind out of his lungs—and he landed heavily on his back, gasping for air and grasping his chest, as though he was suffering a heart attack, which he surely was.

The two assassins immediately scattered, moving swiftly to the departure area for a flight to Zurich that left thirty minutes later.

The first assassinations happened in the last three days of August 1992. The Summer Massacres, they were called afterward by the thoroughly cowed employees of Konevitch Associates.

Andri Kelinichetski, bachelor, bon vivant, and very popular vice president for investor relations, ended up first in the queue. A lifelong insomniac, he left his cramped apartment at two in the morning for a brisk walk in the cool Moscow air to clear the demons from his head. He had made it three blocks from his apartment when three bullets, fired from thirty feet behind his skull, cleared his head, literally. Andri stopped breathing before he hit the cement.

Five hours later, Tanya Nadysheva, divorced mother of

two and a specialist in distressed companies, started up her newly purchased red Volkswagen sedan for the drive to work, triggering a powerful bomb. Her head landed half a block away; she had been operating her fancy new sunroof at the precise instant of detonation.

By ten o'clock that morning, six employees of Konevitch Associates lay in the morgue—one long-distance shooting, one short-distance, a hand grenade attack, one car bombing, one very grisly slit throat, and a notably devout employee who was literally fed a poisoned wafer as he stopped off at his local church for his habitual morning Communion.

Six victims. Six different types of murder. No failed attempts, no survivors, no witnesses. With the exception of the sliced throat and the fatal Communion wafer, the killers—obviously more than one—had struck from a distance, safely and anonymously. No forensic traces were found beyond spent bullets and bomb residue. The particles from the explosive devices were analyzed on the spot by a veteran field technician. In his opinion, the devices were so coarse and simple, virtually any criminal idiot could've built them.

A few hours later, a pair of special police investigators showed up, unannounced, at the headquarters of Konevitch Associates. They flashed badges, announced their purpose with a show of grim expressions, and were ushered hurriedly upstairs. They marched into Alex's office, where they found him and several of his more senior executives assembled, making hasty arrangements for the families of their dead friends and employees, plainly in shock over what had just happened. One executive, Nadia Pleshinko, was blowing snot into a white tissue, unable to stop weeping.

One officer was fat, mustachioed, and late-middle-aged, the other surprisingly young, runway skinny, with a face that looked glum even when he smiled. Laurel and Hardy, they were inevitably nicknamed by the boys at the precinct, a resemblance so glaring that even they celebrated the epithet.

They were both lieutenants with the municipal police, they informed the gathering, here to discuss what had been learned or not about the morning butchery.

"The Mafiya," the fat senior one opened his briefing. "That's who's behind this. It's not just you, it's happening all over Moscow. There have been over sixty murders in the city just this past month. Sixty!" he said, rolling his bloodshot eyes with wearied disgust. "Nearly all were businesspeople, bankers, and one or two news reporters who were getting too close to one of the mobs or to a corrupt politician on their payroll."

Skinny picked up where his partner left off. "Under the old system, the city averaged maybe three murders a month. And that was a bad month. Nearly always angry wives or husbands getting even for an affair or some marital slight or squabble."

"And the Mafiya is behind all these murders?" Alex asked, totally uninterested in a prolonged recounting of Moscow murderography. All that mattered was what happened to *his* people *that* morning. And what might happen tomorrow. Were the killers finished, or just warming up? Were these six the final toll? Or should Alex buy bulletproof vests and begin building thick bunkers for his employees?

A serious nod from both officers and Skinny said, "In the old days they were into drugs, prostitution, the black market, that kind of funny stuff. Capitalism has given them a whole new lease. The big money these days is companies like yours. It's—"

"What do they want?" Alex interrupted.

"Hard to say," Fatty replied with a sad frown. "Usually it's a shakedown. Some variation of a protection or extortion racket. 'Pay us a few million, or give us a cut of the monthly profit, and we'll stop killing your people.' I'm afraid that's the optimistic scenario."

Alex paused for a moment, then reluctantly asked, "And what's the pessimistic one?"

Skinny took over and said, "It could also be that somebody—a competitor perhaps—is paying them to wipe you out. Or maybe to soften you up for an attempted takeover. Either way, they'll keep killing until you're out of business, or until they believe you're ready to meet their terms. These people are ambitious, creative, and vicious." He looked over at Fatty, who offered an approving nod. "For instance," he continued, "they hit a banking company two months ago. Before you could say turnip soup, twelve executives were dead."

"The Mafiya," Alex said, rolling that ugly sound off his lips. "Aren't they organized into families or groups? It's not just one big mob, is it?"

"No, you're right," Skinny told him, warming to the subject. "Only two years ago we could've told you which syndicate was behind this, who headed the group, with an accurate, up-to-date, well-detailed manning and organization chart. These days there are so many mobs..." He trailed off.

He paused for a quick look at their beleaguered faces. "Even the ones we do know about multiply, merge, and divide so fast, we've lost count. They outnumber us, outgun us, and, worse, frankly, they're now smarter than we are."

"Can you protect us?" one of Alex's executives nervously asked, clearly speaking for them all.

It was a good question and the two officers looked at each other. Eventually, and with matched, timid expressions they turned back to Alex and his people. Fatty cleared his throat once or twice. "We can certainly give it our best try. Add more people to the investigation, make inquiries to local stoolies, throw a few uniformed guards outside your headquarters, that sort of thing. We're not in the bodyguard business, though. And frankly, you have too many employees to protect. That bank I mentioned a moment ago, we were doing our best to protect it." He rolled his eyes and sighed. "Twelve dead."

Before they could dwell on that, Skinny looked at Alex and asked, "Have you received any threats? Direct communications in any form from the killers?"

"No, not a word."

This was apparently a bad omen, as both policemen seemed to frown at the same time. As if by hidden cue, Fatty eventually shook his head and spoke up. "Not good. Typically they warn you beforehand. You do this, or we'll do that."

"Sometimes it's Chinese water torture," Skinny threw in, showing off his own mastery of the subject. "Other times it's a sledgehammer, and, to be perfectly frank, this has all the hallmarks of the latter. These people are professionals. They choose how and when to make their approach."

If they were trying to scare Alex and his employees, they were succeeding nicely. A few chairs were pushed back. One or two executives uttered loud groans.

After another quiet pause, Fatty said, "Here's the pattern we're seeing. Number one, they knew the names of your employees, their addresses, and their personal habits. I don't need to tell you what this implies. Your company has been under their eye for a long time, maybe even penetrated from the inside. Who knows how many of your people are on their payroll, or how many of you are targeted for hits. Number two, the potpourri of killing methods is a carefully scripted message in itself—they can kill you however and whenever they want, wherever you are, whatever you're doing."

The two officers continued batting around theories and chilling speculations, oblivious to the sheer horror they were inciting. Alex and his underlings exchanged piercing looks before Alex, with a discomfited shrug, looked away and contemplated a white wall. Nobody needed to say it: resentment cut like a knife through the room. Alex had all those layers of personal protection—those six beefy bodyguards, a private home with the best security systems money could buy, an armored Mercedes limousine, and a lifestyle that kept him off the streets, out of harm's way.

The four senior executives in the room, just like the rest of the employees of Konevitch Associates, were sitting ducks. Totally defenseless. Morgue meat, all of them.

And the cops were right. It took less than a year after the disintegration of the Soviet Union for Moscow to descend into chaos. Brutal murders were a daily event, soldiers were hawking their weapons and ammunition on street corners for a few measly rubles, unemployment had shot through the ceiling. In the clumsy rush to privatize, prices had climbed to dizzying heights, and public services, which had never been decent, deteriorated, then collapsed altogether. A long, fierce winter of misery set in. Hundreds of thousands of Muscovites couldn't afford oil to heat their homes, to buy decent food or clothing, and were turning to crime to make ends meet.

The newspapers were loaded with stories about the self-ennobling extravagances of the newly rich and famous, while hundreds starved or froze to death in Russia's arctic winter. Nobody was going to feel sorry for Konevitch Associates. No matter how many of its well-fed executives were shot, bombed, or chopped up, nobody would waste an ounce of pity. And the drumbeat of news stories about the shining toys and refurbished palaces of the newly rich worked like a tantalizing announcement to the criminals: "Here it is, boys! Come and get it."

When the two officers finished batting around the possibilities, Alex said, in an accusatory tone, "So you can't protect us?"

"To be honest, no," Fatty replied with a sad shake of the head and an earthquake of chin wobbles. "These days, we barely have enough manpower to haul the bodies to the morgue."

"What do you suggest, then?" Alex asked, avoiding the eyes of his executives, who looked ready to dodge from the room and flee for their lives.

"What we tell everybody who asks. Private security, Mr. Konevitch. You have a rich company. You can afford to hire the best."

Skinny looked like he wanted to say more and Alex glanced in his direction. "If you have something to add, we'd like to hear it."

"All right. Off the record. Between us. And just us, please. These are Mafiya people we're talking about. In case you haven't already gotten the message, they're tough, ruthless, and stubborn. But there is somebody who scares the shit out of these guys."

"Go on."

"KGB people. Former KGB people. They and the Mafiya have been at war for fifty years. Remember the old saying 'it takes one to know one'? A lot of highly trained former operatives are now out on the streets, unemployed, desperate for jobs and willing to work hard. Talented people, a lot of them. They have skills, experience, and attitude. To be blunt, the KGB people are even worse than the Mafiya types."

Alex spent a quiet, troubled moment thinking about the officer's suggestion. He had nothing but rotten memories of the KGB and was privately delighted that he had helped put them out of business. They had booted him out of college and nearly destroyed his life. They very nearly destroyed his country. Under communism, the Mafiya were nothing but a nasty irritant, twobit gangsters engaged in shadowy enterprises that barely made a dent. The real mob was the KGB. It turned itself into the world's greatest extortion racket, a mass of faceless thugs who abused their power endlessly, living like spoiled princes while their people suffered in an asylum of terrified poverty.

No, he decided on the spot: not today, not tomorrow, not ever. No matter how bad it got, he would never employ a former KGB person to work in his company.

Fatty read his disapproving expression and withdrew a business card from his pocket that he smoothly slid across the table. "In the event you change your mind, Sergei Golitsin is the man to call. He was the number two in the KGB, a retired three-star general. Whatever you need, believe me, he can take care of."

The next morning, after four more dead employees of Konevitch Associates were scraped off the cement and hauled to the morgue, Alex called Sergei Golitsin.

*   *   *

The door opened loudly and the room filled with noisy voices, a number of people, one or two women and several men, speaking crudely in Russian. Alex had no idea where he was—the car ride had lasted nearly half an hour—a fast trip filled with abrupt, jarring turns probably intended as much to disorient Alex and Elena as to elude any followers. He and Elena were pulled and shoved out of the backseat, then pushed and tugged through a doorway into a building that smelled cloyingly of oil and kerosene. The floor was hard concrete. By the loud echoes of their footsteps, the room was large, cavernous, and mostly empty.

A vacant warehouse, Alex guessed. Or possibly an abandoned garage.

From there, he and Elena were immediately split up and forced into separate rooms. Alex was rushed inside another, smaller room, laid out on what he guessed was a hard table or medical gurney, and the work began. A pair of strong hands untied his shoes, yanked them off his feet, and they landed with a noisy *clumpf* on the floor. A knife skillfully carved off his pants and shirt, leaving him naked except for his Jockeys.

A different pair of stronger hands efficiently clamped his arms and legs tightly with leather straps attached to the sides of the table. Because of the blindfold, he had not a clue what they had done with Elena, where they had taken her. The only thing Alex was sure of was this: it was no coincidence the kidnapping had taken place on one of the few occasions when they traveled together outside Russia, man and wife, on a business trip. This, more than anything, terrified him.

But he squeezed shut his eyes and somehow forced himself to think. Whoever these people were, they had somehow breached, then eliminated his security. Further, the simple yet elaborate kidnapping indicated they had advance knowledge, somehow, that he and Elena were traveling to Budapest. They were waiting for him. They knew his schedule and movements to a tee. And they were professionals—he was sure of this, for whatever it meant, for whatever it was worth.

What kind of professionals, though? Kidnappers out for a fat ransom? Or assassins? That was the urgent question.

They knew he was wondering and left him alone on the gurney to stew and suffer in isolation for nearly half an hour.

Then he heard two sets of footsteps approach, one pair moving lightly, the other heavy, making loud clumps. Probably hard-soled boots. Through the blindfold, he sensed somebody looking down on him, still not speaking, barely breathing. Alex's own breaths were pouring out heavily, his heart racing, his nightmares growing by the second. His mind told him they were allowing the terror to build and he should fight it. His heart would not allow it; he was utterly terrorized.

Without a word or warning, a fist struck him in the midsection; every bit of oxygen in his lungs exploded out of his mouth with a noisy *ooompf*. He sucked for air and tried to say, "What do—" when the fist struck again, this time in his groin. He couldn't even double over or writhe in agony. He screamed, and the beating continued, methodically, without pause, only the sounds of the fists striking against flesh and bone, and Alex howling and groaning in agony.

Vladimir stepped out of the room and slipped off the leather gloves that now were nearly saturated with blood,

Alex's blood. He lifted the phone, and Golitsin, sounding like he was next door and experiencing an orgasm, said, "That was wonderful. Just wonderful. Thank you."

"You heard it all?"

"Every punch, every groan. What a treat. How did he look?"

"In shock, at first. He had not a clue why he was being beaten. Now he is merely miserable and confused. You heard him."

"I certainly did. Any broken bones?" he asked, sounding hopeful.

"A few ribs, I would think. Possibly the leg I banged with a chair. And I tore his left shoulder out of the socket. You must've heard the pop. It was certainly loud enough."

"Ah...I wondered what that was." Golitsin laughed. "As long as you didn't damage his precious right hand."

"No, no, of course not," Vladimir assured him, then waited, knowing Golitsin was calling the shots. If it was another beating, fine, though Vladimir needed at least ten minutes to catch his wind and rest his muscles.

After a moment, Golitsin asked, "Is he still conscious?"

"A little bit less than more. We had to revive him a few times. In twenty minutes or so the bruises will be swollen and his nerve endings will resensitize." He sounded like he'd done this many times.

"Good. Give him twenty minutes to recover, then mark him." There was a long pause before Golitsin stressed, "Slowly, stretch it out for all it's worth."

They were not going to kill him, Alex, in his moments of groggy consciousness, kept telling himself. Between the sounds of his own beating, he heard a voice, a woman's, deep and scornful, issuing occasionally stern reminders to the man torturing him. Soften the blows, she warned. Avoid damaging important organs, she reminded him. Twice she had loudly snarled that he had better stop choking Alex before their precious hostage had to be hauled out in a box.

So they needed him alive. They wouldn't kill him. They wanted something from him, and they would keep him breathing until they had it; whatever it was.

Then they might kill him.

The door opened loudly again, and two sets of footsteps approached. Same two pairs of feet, Alex thought, one light, one heavy. Were they going to beat him again? He totally forgot his earlier reasoning and wondered, maybe they *were* going to kill him?

The blindfold was ripped from his head. He blinked a few times. "What do you want?" he croaked, throat parched. No answer, not a peep. He tried to focus his eyes, which were blurry and unfocused though he was positive the hazy shapes before him were the same man and woman from the taxi. And probably the same pair who had inflicted the brutal beating.

"Please. Just tell me what you want."

The man, Vladimir, he had heard him called, bent down over his face, smiled, squeezed open his lids, and studied his pupils a moment. Vladimir then took two thick leather straps and, one at a time, stretched them across Alex's chest, strung them underneath the table, fastened them as he would a belt, and tightened them enough that they bit painfully into Alex's skin. Next he held something before his face—a handheld device. A machine of some sort. Oddly enough, it looked like a compact traveling iron for pressing clothes. "See this?" he asked Alex.

"Yes ... what is it?"

"You'll learn in a moment."

"Where's Elena?" Alex demanded.

Vladimir laughed.

"Please," Alex pleaded. "Leave her out of this. She's done nothing to you."

"But you have," Vladimir informed him with a mean smile.

"I don't even know you." Sensing it was the wrong thing to say, Alex suggested, a little hopefully, "If it's money, let's agree on a price. Let her go. Keep me. She'll make sure you get paid."

"Are you proud of what you did?" Vladimir asked, backing away. He spit on the iron and enjoyed the angry hiss.

"I don't know what you're talking about."

The woman spoke up and said, "Most of us are former KGB. Career people, patriotic servants who protected Mother Russia. You ruined our lives."

"How?" Alex asked.

"You know how. You fed millions to Yeltsin and destroyed our homeland."

"How do you know about this?"

"We know all about you, Alex Konevitch. We've watched you for years. Watched you undermine our country. Watched you become rich off the spoils. Now it's time to return the favor."

Alex closed his eyes. Things had just gone from bad to worse. Not only did they know him, they knew *about* him. A simple kidnapping was bad enough. This was revenge on top of it, and both Vladimir and Katya allowed Alex a few moments to contemplate how bad this was going to get.

Vladimir held up the iron so they could jointly inspect it; the metal undertray was red-hot, glowing fiercely in the dimly lit room. He held it before Alex's face. "American cowboys branded their cattle. I hope you don't mind, but now we will brand you."

Without another word, Vladimir slipped a pair of industrial earphones over his head, thick black rubber gloves over his hands, then with a steady hand lowered the iron slowly toward Alex's chest. Watching it move closer, Alex squirmed and tried to evade it with all his might; the new belts totally immobilized him. The first hot prick of the iron seared the tender flesh above his left nipple— Vladimir used the recently sharpened edges of the iron and glided it slowly and skillfully around his skin.

Alex screamed and Vladimir pressed down firmly, though not too hard, etching a careful pattern: a long curve first, then another curve, meticulously connecting them into the shape of a sickle. The stench of burning flesh filled the room. Next, he began drawing a squarish shape—completing the hammer and sickle, the symbol of the once feared and mighty, now historically expired Soviet Union. Vladimir had done this before; this was obvious. Just as obviously, he was the kind of artisan who reveled in his work. The entire process lasted thirty minutes. Alex screamed until he went hoarse, piercing shrieks that echoed and bounced around the warehouse.

Katya stood and tried to watch, then, after two minutes, horrified, she gave up and fled.

5

By 3:30, Eugene Daniels was quaffing down the final dregs of his third Bavarian brew, a special, thick dunkel beer produced seasonally without preservatives that was totally unavailable in the States. Across the table, his wife, Maria, was stingily nursing her second wine, a Georgian pinot she had just explained, for the second time, with an excellent bouquet, overly subtle perhaps, but with fine, lingering legs and other insufferable claptrap she had obviously lifted from one of those snobbish wine books. How could anybody make so much of squished grapes? An attractive Hungarian waitress approached the table and, while Eugene wasn't looking, Maria quietly waved her off.

She toyed with the stem of her wineglass and reminded her husband, "Business meetings are best conducted sober."

"If Alex wanted me sober, he'd be here on time."

"Maybe he has something up his sleeve. Hundreds of millions are at stake, Eugene. Maybe he wants you loaded and stupid before he arrives." And maybe he's succeeding beyond his wildest dream, she thought and smiled coldly.

"You don't know Alex, obviously."

Rather than risk another squabble, Maria lifted a finely plucked eyebrow and insisted with a disapproving frown, "All the same, switch to coffee."

Eugene ignored this and took a long sip of beer. He checked his watch for the thirtieth time, then repeated the same thing he had said at least twenty times. "I've never known Alex to be late. He's punctual to a fault. Always."

"Maybe he has a Russian watch. I know for a fact, their craftsmanship is awful."

He was tempted to say: How would you know, you stupid spoiled twit? but swallowed the sentiment and instead noted, "No, something's wrong. I smell it."

"Yes, you're right. This whole thing is dreadfully wrong. We flew all the way from New York, he only had to come from Moscow, we're here, and he's not. This is rude and unprofessional. We should leave."

Eugene stared hard at his wife and fought the urge to stuff a napkin down her throat. Wife number four, actually—and without question, the biggest mistake of all. He was still on his third wife and making a decent go of it when Maria, a buxom brunette half his age and with a penchant for tight leather miniskirts, became his secretary. He'd chased her around the desk a few times, but not too many before she hit the brakes and made the pursuit pay off.

When it got out—with more than a little assistance from Maria, he only belatedly and after the fact realized—Wife Three stomped off into the sunset with a fifty million settlement and that big, ostentatious mansion in the Hamptons to quell her hurt pride. Word was she now had a shiny new red Rolls and a good-looking cabana boy to help her through the emotional relapses.

The house and money had been bad enough. What Eugene most sorely regretted was losing the one really capable secretary he ever had. Maria was pushy, curt, and anal, keeping him organized and punctual, and cleaning